"Don't move."

Terrified, Nora froze, staring at the letter she now realized was not a letter at all.

Seth eased the envelope out of Nora's fingers and walked as steadily as he could away from Nora. "Get Jude," he instructed.

Nora ran inside and returned a moment later with her brother.

Jude pushed Nora back toward the building, eyes riveted on Seth. "Bomb squad's on its way but it will be a while. Can you put it down?"

Seth did, lowering it millimeter by excruciating millimeter down onto the pavement.

Nora stood, lip between her teeth, trembling. When Seth joined them, he reached a hand to her. She took it, holding onto his strong fingers. "How...how did you know that was a bomb?"

He smiled grimly. "Heavy envelope, grease stains, bump where the trigger is hidden inside. Military service makes you savvy." He paused. "And the fact that someone recently threatened your life."

Nora's grip tightened before she let go and hugged herself. He knew what she was thinking and he wondered too. Why did someone want her dead?

Dana Mentink is a nationally bestselling author.
She has been honored to win two Carol Awards, a
HOLT Medallion and an RT Reviewers' Choice Best Book
Award. She's authored more than thirty novels to date
for Love Inspired Suspense and Harlequin Heartwarming.
Dana loves feedback from her readers. Contact her at
danamentink.com.

Visit the Author Profile page at LoveInspired.com for more titles.

CHRISTMAS CRIME COVER-UP

DANA MENTINK

LOVE INSPIRED SUSPENSE
INSPIRATIONAL ROMANCE

LOVE INSPIRED® SUSPENSE
INSPIRATIONAL ROMANCE

ISBN-13: 978-1-335-58812-8

Christmas Crime Cover-Up

Recycling programs for this product may not exist in your area.

For questions and comments about the quality of this book, please contact us at CustomerService@Harlequin.com.

Love Inspired
22 Adelaide St. West, 41st Floor
Toronto, Ontario M5H 4E3, Canada
www.LoveInspired.com

Printed in U.S.A.

Brethren, I count not myself to have apprehended:
but this one thing I do, forgetting those things
which are behind, and reaching forth unto those things
which are before, I press toward the mark
for the prize of the high calling of God in Christ Jesus.
—*Philippians* 3:13-14

To Donna in Florida, my prayer pal and sister.

ONE

Nora Duke gripped the binoculars as the winter drizzle beaded her baseball cap. Lying facedown on a small perch of rock, she scoured the gritty path below them, pressed in by boulders on one side and plunging to the riverbank on the other. The December chill numbing her fingers was familiar, as if the desert climate patterns would be forever baked into her cells no matter how far she ran from Furnace Falls in Death Valley. Creepy thought.

She'd worn a dark hat, insulated jacket and sturdy boots. Still, her hands stiffened with cold as the time ticked away, taking her patience with it. There was barely another hour before sunset to accomplish the mission. She held the binoculars tighter. "Come on, come on. Where are you?" she whispered.

An unexpected noise behind made her flinch. The snap of a twig? Her friend Felicia returning from their truck? Probably just a creature prowling by the water. The Amargosa River bubbled its way to the surface in a few areas, like nearby Beatty and the Amargosa Canyon where she now found herself…and where they'd expected to find their quarry. But the sneaky feral donkey had traversed an access road toward the nearby Sandy Ranch Date Farm. The wily critter had escaped the earlier efforts of the Big Valley Horse and Donkey Rescue dispatched from Colorado where she and Felicia worked. They were the "cleanup hitters" so to speak, because the rest of the team was now back in Ouray tending the herd of fifteen successfully captured donkeys.

"The buck stops here," Nora muttered. "Gonna capture you for your own good, baby."

The adorable non-native donkeys would quickly reproduce to the point of starvation if they weren't captured and rehomed. Made sense that the rogue female would head for the date farm. There was a small corral there where the owner, Zane Freeman, kept a few horses. That meant a nice, deep, water trough, plenty of hay and shelter from the rain. Donkeys were not fans of getting wet.

Heedless of the drizzle, Felicia tiptoed next to her and sat down cross-legged on a rock. Nora heard the crinkling of a wrapper.

"Can't you wait until we catch her?" Nora

said. "She might hear you. Sound travels in the desert, you know."

Felicia huffed out an unconcerned breath and spoke around a bite of candy. "I know, I grew up here too, remember? That donkey has her mind on other things besides my snack, and I haven't eaten since we left the diner this morning. Besides, who knows how long this could take?" She wiggled a candy bar in front of the binocular lenses. "Want one? It's got nougat and nuts and loads of sugar and calories. Perfection."

Nora smiled. Felicia's sweet tooth was legendary. "No thanks. We're gonna wrap this up quick. Seth will give us a location as soon as he gets his drone in the air."

Felicia pulled the hood down low over her puff of rain-frizzed hair. "Seth's a sweetheart. So nice of him to call us when he spotted the donkey in the first place. Handsome too. His scar makes him look rugged, don't you think?"

Nora heard the calculation in the tone. Yes, Seth Castillo was handsome, and he'd come across as a good guy in their numerous phone calls and Zoom meetings, but Nora wasn't interested in anyone in this town. She could only hope Seth hadn't lived in the area long enough to know about her past. Her heart tripped, imagining what he might think of her. *He's a stranger*, she reminded herself. Odd the way it felt as if she'd known him for much longer than the weeks they'd spent chatting via their computer.

She realized her friend was waiting for an answer.

"Don't get your matchmaking gears in motion. I'm out of Furnace Falls the moment we capture this jenny and the vet gives her the all clear." Nora paused. "You too?" She held her breath.

Felicia sighed. "I told Mom I'd stay for a few days after I help you capture the jenny. Maybe through Christmas. Things are better with her, and it'd be so amazing if we could finally put the past behind us this time," she said. "We have some good memories from Furnace Falls too, remember. It wasn't all a catastrophe. There are nice people here."

One in particular for Felicia, namely her high school crush Zane Freeman. Maybe Felicia would restart her life here, without Nora. The thought formed like a hard lump in her throat.

Felicia swallowed a bite of candy. "When we talked on the phone last week, Zane said he was happy to hear from me, couldn't wait to connect again while I was in town chasing donkeys and visiting Mom." She paused.

"Those were his exact words. *I can't wait.*" Her soft smile was almost lost in growing shadows from the towering pile of rock that sheltered them.

Nora's phone buzzed. She shielded it with her hand and answered.

"This is like looking for a donkey in a haystack," Seth joked.

Nora could not resist a chuckle. The guy was charming, she had to admit. As the co-owner of the Rocking Horse Ranch, he had the perfect setup to house the wayward donkey until it was cleared by a vet to travel back to Colorado. An animal lover through and through, clearly. He'd bent over backward to assist in the capture too. "If we had a haystack, she'd be chowing down there right now."

"I should have thought to bring one. You two need anything? I've got coffee in my Bronco. I brought extra cups in case this went on for a while."

He'd brought coffee for them? The gesture kindled a warm feeling that she immediately shook off. "We're okay," she said before Felicia could chime in. "Can you see anything?"

"Just getting the drone up. Give me a second." There was a scuffling noise. "Flying drones is tricky...and expensive if I'm the one at the controls."

"Crashed a few?"

"How did you know?"

"Wild guess. You said you're an army veteran. I assume piloting wasn't your bag."

"Nope. Combat medic."

Felicia's eyes widened and she smiled slyly. *Combat medic*, she mouthed. *How cool.*

Nora tried to ignore her as Seth continued.

"While I was learning how to fly drones, I hung one in a tree and spooked a horse with another. Guy who co-owns the ranch with me threatened to shoot down my drone if I continued to practice."

She stifled a giggle. "Alarming."

"No worries. I don't take defeat easily. Ah. Here we go. Drone's up. Give me a minute to focus."

Her attention was snagged by a sound behind them. "What was that?" she asked Felicia.

"I didn't hear anything." Felicia set about unwrapping the second candy bar.

"You two okay over there?" Seth asked.

"Yes," Nora said, mildly annoyed. She didn't need coffee nor coddling. "I thought I heard… Never mind. What do you have on the donkey?"

"Rain is affecting visibility, but… Oh hey, lookie-loo," he said.

Seth was probably the only man she'd ever

heard use that particular phrase. Somehow it suited him.

"Got a view of our missing burro," he said. "Sure enough, she's heading right for the corral at the date ranch."

"Perfect. I'll have Felicia call Zane and tell him we'll trap her there and load her into the trailer."

"Sounds like a plan. I've got a pen all ready for her at the Rocking Horse, and Doc's on call to do the exam."

Nora let out a puff of air. The mission was almost accomplished. Good thing too, since it was now officially dark, except for the glow of the crescent moon that occasionally appeared between the clouds. She shot a look at Felicia, who was silhouetted by silver light. She stood staring not down toward the date farm but away into the wild land behind them. Her hand was stopped halfway to her mouth, holding the partially eaten candy bar.

"What is it?" Nora said.

"So weird," she said, still staring. "I thought I saw…"

A high buzzing sound carried over the rain. At first Nora's brain could not identify it. Death Valley, immense and mostly wild, was a place insulated from the constant thrum of metropolitan noise. But this was a sound from her youth, before everything had gone terribly awry. It was an auditory snapshot of her and her brother, side by side, tearing through the sand dunes on his all-terrain vehicle, fifteen years old to her five, hot wind blasting their faces. The memory was lost as her body reacted, reaching for Felicia the moment the oncoming headlights blazed up from the riverbank.

Seth Castillo watched the video feed from the drone, trying to make sense of it. "What's going on, Nora?" he snapped, but all he heard was a crunch. Her phone falling? He tried to sort out what he was seeing, to fight through the slow processing that sometimes affected him from the head injury he'd received a little more than a year before. Blazing lights jumped in tandem on his drone monitor; headlights where they shouldn't be.

He dropped the drone controls and leapt into his battered Bronco, cranking it to life. His position at the knoll due north of the date farm was no more than five minutes from Nora and Felicia's location. But five minutes was more than enough time to change a life forever, he knew. The quick movements aggravated the perpetual throb in his skull where the bullet had plowed through muscle and bone. Urging the Bronco as fast as he dared on the grit-strewn trail, he barreled toward the river.

Who would be in an ATV at this hour? Someone out for a ride, unknowingly endangering the women? Not a chance. His violent injury had incinerated most of his naïveté in a way that even his time in the army hadn't. This was no accident. Nora and Felicia were targets. Why, he could not spare a moment to ponder.

One hand grappling the wheel, he cranked down the window with the other. At first all he caught was the pattering rain, until a cry cut through the night, high and shrill. A woman's terrified scream. The sound ricocheted off the riverbank and the rocks beyond, making it impossible to locate the source.

Heart slamming against his ribs, he forced himself to brake to a stop. Shoving his head outside into the rain, he strained to hear, praying he would find the women in time. A gleam of light flickered twenty yards to his right, electrifying him. He spun the wheel and plowed the Bronco directly at it. The rear of an ATV came into view yards behind a woman silhouetted in the glare. Nora? Felicia? She was running, stumbling over the irregular ground as the driver closed the gap between them. Seth goosed the gas and the Bronco bucked over dips and gullies. The woman was attempting to get to the thicket of willows and mesquite that flanked the river. A dip thrust the Bronco up until it dropped down with a teeth-cracking jolt, nearly yanking the wheel from his hands.

You can do this, Seth. Just like the old days when you had those lightning-quick reflexes, right?

A hunk of granite loomed on the ground in the glare of his headlights. He jerked the wheel to prevent the rock from ripping through the front axle. When he rejoined the pursuit, the ATV was shooting straight for the thicket but the dark prevented him seeing anything further. Was the woman still there? Had she reached the sheltering branches? Been crushed by the pursuer? The ATV's rear license plate was smeared with mud, not that he could have given the numbers much attention anyway.

Where are you, Nora? Felicia? There. His heart leapt as he caught a momentary glimpse of a hand thrown up as if to ward off a blow. The woman's pace had slowed, bogged by the muddy ground or fatigue. Still the ATV dogged her, close enough now that the front tires were only a couple of feet away.

"You're almost to the trees," he shouted uselessly. The roaring vehicle was much more mobile than Seth's Bronco, but even that four-wheeler wouldn't successfully navigate through the thicket. But the woman was slowing, faltering, and he feared she did not have the stamina to make it to safety.

All right then. We'll do this the hard way. He pressed the gas and caught up with the ATV, smacking the rear left tire. It shimmied and veered away from the trees. Seth stuck close, trying to connect with the ATV again, but the vehicle was nimble and the driver obviously experienced at off-roading. He zoomed away, rumbling back up to the gravel road and roaring off.

Seth watched him go, wiping the sweat from his forehead. He didn't trust that the encounter was over. He had to get to Nora and Felicia before the attacker regrouped.

He yanked the Bronco into a tight turn and reversed course to where he'd seen the woman near the thicket. He left the engine idling and got out.

"Nora, Felicia," he shouted. "It's Seth."

There was no answer save his own labored breaths. He called and texted Nora's phone. No response. Then he called 9-1-1. The dispatcher told him Chief Jude Duke would respond. But would it be too late?

Phone flashlight activated, he shoved his way through the biggest gap in the branches.

"It's Seth. Where are you?" he shouted into the darkness.

A trembling in the bushes to his left made him spin around. The woman he had only seen on Zoom sitting next to Nora stumbled forward. Felicia. Her face was scratched and bleeding, her light-colored hair tangled. The knee of her jeans was torn, exposing a moist gleam that was probably blood. "Felicia?" He moved for her, grabbing her arm as she threatened to collapse. "I'm Seth Castillo. I don't know what happened here, but I'm going to get you someplace safe, okay?"

She nodded, her lips pinched together and her breaths coming in panicked puffs through her nostrils. When he gently took her arm, her fingers sunk deeply into his skin. "He…he tried to kill us."

Seth urged her away from the thicket that had saved her life. "You're safe now. Where's Nora?"

"What?"

"Nora, where is she?"

Felicia's eyes went round with horror. "I thought you found her before me."

His nerves iced over. Where was Nora? Not able to reply to texts or calls. No answer to his shouts. "I didn't see her," he said slowly, trying to keep his tone reassuring as he guided Felicia to the Bronco. "But we'll find her. She's probably hiding and afraid to come out." His stomach muscles balled into knots. Nora didn't seem to be a woman who would be paralyzed by fear.

Then why hadn't she responded?

Comforting Felicia as best as he could, he prayed they would find Nora alive.

Nora held the cramp in her side, gasping for breath. Fear teased goose bumps on her skin. She had no idea how she'd managed to outrun the murderous ATV and reach shelter behind a rocky outcropping. She patted her pockets again for her cell phone. It must have fallen out. With no way to contact Felicia or Seth, the best course of action was to get back to her vehicle and find them.

She strained to identify the shadowed landscape around her to orient herself. There, just ahead, she noticed the faint gleam of the gravel road. Carefully, she made her way back to the truck.

She had to find Felicia. One moment, she was gripping her sleeve as they stumbled toward the rocks, and the next, her friend was gone and the ATV had rolled out of view. Giving up the chase? She didn't think so. Pursuing Felicia? Her mouth went dry.

Fear pounded hard as she yanked open the truck door and pulled out the rifle she kept in the back seat. She was a good shot, but rain and darkness and fear was a recipe for a shooting disaster. Plus, this was not a wild animal attack. This was a deliberate human assault.

She pulled the truck onto the gravel road, keeping it at a slow creep, headlights off. Not like she had achieved stealth mode. The attached animal trailer creaked and rattled behind the truck. She searched through the rain-soaked darkness, knowing hazards were all around, the plunging slope nearby, the riverbank. What if Felicia was running through the night, heedless of the dangers? What if she'd already been struck by the ATV and was lying wounded and broken? She surged ahead.

Had Seth come to help? Would he be a target too? She pictured his genial smile, wide green eyes and curly hair that framed his scarred forehead.

I don't take defeat easily.

Was it just talk or a reflection of his character? She didn't know Seth well enough to judge. Would he have called for help and sat tight or come to assist them? *He'll help.* She didn't know how she knew that about Seth, but she did.

Drizzle spattered her cheeks as she leaned

out the window to listen. No noise surfaced save the soft pattering of rain and the breeze churning the long grasses. Where was Felicia?

Think, Nora. You can track animals, you can find Felicia.

She refocused. It was time to put her skills to work.

She stopped the truck and, after snagging a penlight from the glove box, she scurried to the softer earth on the shoulder. She bent down and played the light over the ground. The sandy surface was rutted in places where the soil had become sodden by winter rains and traffic to and from the date farm. A few deep troughs showed evidence that a motorcycle had passed by recently. Looking more closely, she saw something reflect the light. A half-eaten candy bar tucked in a silver wrapper. "All right," she muttered. "Now we're getting somewhere."

The candy bar lay on the riverbank side of the road. Felicia must have run for cover into the thicket. Her friend was quick and agile, she'd made it to safety, Nora told herself. She had to. Any other possibilities were intolerable. Felicia was the sister Nora had never had and always longed for. A proper sister, who saw through all Nora's outbursts and posturing and understood what lay beneath. A sibling who would never cast her out.

Nora flicked off the light when the ATV appeared at the turn in the road, fifty feet behind her, its headlights off.

Scrambling to the truck, she leapt into the driver's seat and hit the gas, the trailer bucking and rattling in protest as Nora hurtled along. Behind her, the ATV's engine noise grew louder, and she knew she was losing ground. The truth came home in a sickening rush. There was no way she could outrun the ATV and if it caught her, she wouldn't get away alive.

Who was it and why were they after Nora and Felicia? They were on public land, innocently trying to capture a needy donkey.

Rage flashed through her body. Nora detested being scared. She'd lost everything—her family, her faith, her friends—but she'd promised herself she would never be beaten by fear. Ever. Her energy turned to steely determination. If she wasn't going to win the race, she'd figure out how to survive it and get to Felicia.

Mentally she scrolled through the drone footage Seth had supplied to plan the donkey capture. Around the next bend, she recalled there was a small bridge that spanned the meandering creek, a narrow stone structure that could accommodate only one vehicle at a time. The bridge would be a bottleneck, like when they funneled the wild donkeys through pinch points in order to capture them. The plan she came up with was reckless but she had no alternative. Whoever was stalking them was going to answer for it.

At this point, her mother would have dropped to her knees and prayed. No way would Nora waste time with that. Prayers were for people who needed saving. Nora intended to do the saving herself.

"All right, ATV Guy. Let's see what you got." She pressed the gas and shot toward the bridge. She remembered that the river deepened at that point, more than twelve feet thanks to the winter rains. She'd make her stand there.

Bits of sand and grit rattled against the undercarriage and finally the bridge came into view. It was small, no more than fifteen feet across. Her nerves tightened, her breath coming fast. If she'd made a mistake, there was no going back.

Rattling onto the bridge, she got to the apex, put the truck in Park and flung open the door. The ATV driver had still not turned on its headlights. Darkness was her friend. Once the ATV was on the bridge with her truck and trailer blocking the way, there was no chance for it to maneuver off, except to back up. And she'd be waiting.

Keeping low under the cover of the stone wall, Nora grabbed the rifle and tossed it down onto the muddy bank under the bridge. With one last look back at the ATV, she crawled onto the edge.

Ambush time, she thought as she pushed off into the darkness.

TWO

Seth tugged the wheel and turned onto the raised access road toward the bridge where he'd caught the sound of an ATV. Or was it a truck? Both, he realized as he saw the truck and trailer stopped on the bridge and the ATV closing in from behind. He felt Felicia's fear rise along with his own. Why had Nora stopped on the bridge? A shadow peeled away from the stone arch. He blinked hard. His eyes must have deceived him. He thought he'd seen...

"She jumped," Felicia gasped, gripping his wrist so hard her nails cut into his skin. "Nora jumped from that bridge."

Jumped. The word thudded against his unbelieving brain. He really had witnessed her dropping feetfirst over the side. Was the water deep enough? Why hadn't she kept driving, gotten herself to safety?

A checklist from his days in the medical corps scrolled through his thoughts. Shock, spinal compression, impact injury, extremity wounds, blood loss… He blinked the thoughts away as his mind put the pieces together. Her actions had been purposeful, calculating. Nora hadn't leapt in blind panic. She'd had a plan to lead the ATV into a trap. When the driver got out to approach the truck, she'd have climbed back up the bank and pinned him down.

A half smile crept across his face. Who was this woman? But there was no time to process what he'd just witnessed. The attacker must have sensed Nora's intention because the ATV was backing away from the bridge at dizzying speed. Seth shoved the Bronco into gear.

"Look out," Felicia cried.

Too late. There was no way he was going to avoid a crash.

"Hold on," he shouted. Five feet from impact. He tried to turn enough that it would not be a head-on blow, but the tires skidded, searching for traction.

Four feet…

As if in a dream, he saw Nora surge up the top of the riverbank, a dark silhouette. He watched her level the rifle at her shoulder and squeeze off a shot. The noise jolted him; the memory of a previous shooter's bullet plowing through his front windshield and into his skull. But this bullet found its target in the

ATV, the front tire exploding with an audible pop. It wobbled, but the driver was too close, less than three feet from Seth's fender. He tensed against the seat belt, teeth clenched for what would happen next. After a surreal, stretched-out moment, the ATV smashed into them, the impact like a shockwave, throwing them both back against the seats. Metal crumpled, the side window cracked. His vehicle was slammed sideways.

Felicia screamed.

As the ATV ripped around them and lurched off into the darkness, its tire flapping, a new threat became clear. Their vehicle was sliding toward the riverbank. Dizzied by the impact, he fought to stop the Bronco. If he didn't, they would catapult into the river.

"Seth!" Felicia gasped.

There was no safe way for her to jump from the vehicle. Their only chance was him.

Teeth gritted, he eased the wheel into the skid, praying they were not close to the edge of the bank and that Nora was out of the way. The moments crept by in slow motion as the tires shimmied across the slick ground until, finally, they began to slow and he was able to bring the Bronco to a stop. Panting, he peered out the cracked driver's window. Their left front tire was six inches from the edge of the bank.

Thank you, Lord.

"Oh wow," Felicia squeaked.

"That pretty much covers it for me too," he managed to huff, wiping the sweat from his brow. "You hurt?"

She shook her head. "You?"

"No." Now to get to Nora. He reached to shove the door open when Felicia called out.

"There she is."

Nora sprinted toward the Bronco, a rifle clutched under her arm. Felicia leaned over the back seat and flung open the door.

"Nora," she said, voice cracking. "I can't believe you did that."

Seth twisted around. She didn't seem to be bleeding and she hadn't been limping.

"Are you two okay?" Nora said, the fringe of bangs plastered onto her wet face.

Felicia nodded. "Seth found me."

"What about you?" he said. "You jumped from the bridge…"

She waved off his concern. "I'm fine. Let's go," she ordered Seth, pointing in the direction the ATV had taken. "We can run him down. He's got a shredded tire."

Somehow, he wasn't surprised at her command. He shook his head. "Not safe. Cops are rolling. We'll wait for help."

She flashed blazing eyes on him. "Seth, he's going to get away."

"The risk isn't worth it."

"Worth it?" She gaped. "Whoever that is tried to kill us."

"And if we go tearing off in the dark, we just might give him another shot at it, or finish the job for him," Seth said calmly. He could feel her hot anger flaming over him. She was stubborn, fiery. He countered the way he'd learned to do long ago as a medic. His role was to calm, deescalate, save lives. "The police are trained. We're ill-equipped amateurs."

"So you want to let him go?" She fired off the words like a barrage of buckshot.

"No, I don't. But what I want more is to keep you two safe."

Her hand squeezed into a fist atop her thigh. "Seth, if you don't move this car, I'll go after him myself, on foot."

Her face was eerily beautiful, her resolution sizzling like a bolt of lightning between them, which pulsed his nerves. "Nora," he said, his tone serene as a windless desert morning, "this situation is a soup sandwich."

"A what?" Felicia said. "You can't make a sandwich out of soup."

"Exactly," he said. "Imagine the mess."

Nora was about to retort when he pointed a

finger out the window. "It's dark, there's someone out there who knows this area better than we do, and you're both cold, wet and susceptible to shock. We drive to a spot near the main road with good visibility and wait for the police. We don't run around trying to eat a soup sandwich."

"This is cowardice," Nora said through gritted teeth.

He absorbed the insult, not allowing the arrow to hit home as he flashed back in time. The shout of "Corpsman up!" brought him running through the remnants of a destroyed Humvee as the team poured out to provide cover fire. He couldn't remember the soldier's name. George? Jeff? But he'd never forget those frightened eyes, dark as the shifting shadows that cloaked them now. "Am I gonna make it, Doc?" Seth had forced a hopefulness he had not felt, a calm message of reassurance as the shouting and gunfire rattled and clanged around them. "Gonna take care of you, man. Don't you worry."

The wounded soldier had flashed a wobbly smile. "Soup sandwich out here, right?" he'd said, mouth tightening in pain.

Another smile from Seth as he'd tried in vain to stop the bleeding. "You know it, brother."

Cowardice was an unfair label, but Seth

would take it, if it meant getting the women out safely. He looked back at her stony gaze, which he knew from their Zoom meetings was the deepest navy blue. "You can call it cowardice if it's easier for you to take."

"Nora, he's right," Felicia said quietly, reaching to squeeze her shoulder.

She beamed a look of fury on him, slumping against the seat. "Can you at least put the drone up? Track his location?"

Seth felt the flush of embarrassment. "I dropped the controller when I ran to help you." He actually heard her teeth grind together. Maybe he should have thought to pack away the drone and controls before he'd launched into rescue mode. No help for it now.

When he was convinced she wasn't going to ignore his advice and leap out, he drove his battered Bronco to higher ground, the junction of the main highway and the road to the date farm. He kept the engine running.

Just in case whoever tried to kill them came back to finish his mission.

Nora's fury ebbed as the minutes ticked by while they waited near the main road. Dread took its place as she considered what lay ahead. The police, her brother Jude. Suddenly she felt chilled to the bone in spite of the blanket Seth had given her. *Go on the offense. Don't let anyone get the upper hand on you, especially not Jude.* She hopped out of the truck as she saw the sheriff's car speeding to meet them, its lights on but no siren. Braced for what was to come, she was mortified to find her whole body trembling.

It was not simply that she was wet and cold and reeling from the ATV attack. It was the uniformed man who got out of the car to face her, tall, muscular, self-assured. His expression was unreadable; a face she'd peeked at online during those moments in the last ten years when she'd been so desperate for family. She'd known Jude had become an Inyo County sheriff from those painful internet checks, and she'd found out when he'd been named chief of Furnace Falls. Her social media poking was a silly weakness she'd never admit to, since she was positive he'd never checked her status.

She wanted to speak first, to show her strength by making the first move down this painful path, but the words stuck in her throat.

Seth and Felicia climbed out. "Chief, am I glad to see you here," Seth said.

Jude shot a curious look at Nora. "Where else would I be when there's an ATV'er wreaking havoc?" he said with a polite smile. "Injuries? Should I roll an ambulance?"

Seth declined the offer and gave Jude a quick retelling of what had happened.

Jude listened without interruption, though his eyebrows shot up at the jumping-from-the-bridge part. "Bold," he said, his gaze still indicating he was trying to place Nora. The darkness and her soggy state delayed the light bulb moment.

She let the comment hang without a reply until he gave up waiting and spoke again. "I've got a unit en route and we'll comb the area." He paused. "Let me get your personal details."

Her stomach contracted. *Here we go.*

"Felicia Tennison." Her friend spoke first and Jude cocked his chin at her. "I know you. In high school you were my sister's best friend."

Nora gulped in a breath. Might as well get it over with. "She still is."

Jude's eyes shifted to hers and she saw them narrow as they recognized her. The air seemed to smother her as the seconds ticked between them.

She felt Seth looking at her too; differently now that he'd caught on. "I didn't catch your last name before," he said. "You didn't mention you had kinfolk in town."

"So it's Nora now?" Jude asked. "What happened to Sadie?"

"I decided to use my middle name, but that has nothing to do with this situation." Did she sound defensive? Probably, even though she was completely innocent…this time.

"Doesn't it?" Jude's face was impassive, like granite.

She raised her chin. "I go by Nora now. I'm here trying to trap a donkey and I intend to leave as soon as humanly possible. I have no idea why someone would attack us, but he may still be down there. I wanted to go search but Seth overruled me."

"Thanks, Seth," Jude said. "For looking out for them."

Patronizing. "I don't need someone to look out for me."

Jude's mouth twisted into a smile that wasn't. "That right?"

There was a universe of disdain in those two words. Fury and despair battled inside her but she could not produce a reply. Teeth clenched, she looked away.

Seth cleared his throat. "Jude," he said softly, "there's obviously some family stuff here, which isn't my business, but these women have been through the wringer. Let me take them back to their hotel."

Felicia sighed. "We didn't book a hotel. Nora

was going to arrange something in Beatty and I promised to stay at my mom's."

"I...didn't get around to making a reservation," Nora said. Because she desperately didn't want to stay. But Felicia deserved to see her mother and try to reconnect with Zane. Just because Furnace Falls was a no-man's-land for Nora didn't mean it had to remain that way for Felicia.

Jude shifted, his gun belt creaking.

"No problem about the hotel," Seth said. "We've got a trailer set up on the Rocking Horse. We're trying to encourage that 'come stay on the ranch and pretend to be a cowboy' thing. It's unoccupied right now while I finish remodeling it, but it's furnished and there's electricity and water and everything. You're both welcome to stay there."

"That's super nice," Felicia said. "We still gotta catch that donkey tomorrow, but like I said, I promised to stay with my mom." She hesitated. "Um, that won't work for Nora, though."

No, it wouldn't. "It's okay," Nora said with forced cheer. "I'll find a room."

"Not in Furnace Falls. The Hotsprings Hotel is booked up for a Christmas golf tournament." Jude twirled the pen over and over in his hand until she wanted to snatch it away from him. "Might be a room in Beatty left."

Seth smiled, as if they weren't standing there in the world's most awkward family re-union. "No need for that when there's a fab-ulous trailer available for free. How about it, Nora? Spend the night and you can check out the digs I've set up."

No, Nora wanted to say. *I can't stay in this town any longer.* But she would endure any-thing at that moment to get away from Jude's calculating stare. As he stood there, she could see his mental wheels spinning.

"All right," she said to Seth. "I'd appreciate it. Thank you."

They heard the sound of trotting hooves and a man appeared astride a painted horse. His dark eyes widened under his cowboy hat as he approached. "Are you all okay?"

Jude greeted him. "Appears there's been a problem near your property, Mr. Freeman."

"Call me Zane," he said, dismounting and catching the reins. Sliding off his hat, he re-vealed a thick head of light-colored hair. Zane was heavier than Nora remembered, his cheeks fuller and darkened with a couple days' worth of scruff, and there were lines bracketing his mouth and grooving his forehead, but he'd held on to his high school charm. The desert sun took its toll, she thought, no matter how much sunscreen a person wore.

Zane shook hands with Seth and Nora. When he got to Felicia, his smile was shyer, clasping her palm between both his and squeezing. "Good to see you, Felicia. I was worried when I heard a gunshot so I saddled a horse and came to check it out." After a moment, he let go.

Nora suspected her friend was blushing. Felicia reached up to tuck her tousled curls behind her ear. Surreptitiously, she stood taller and straightened her jacket. "It's been a weird night, but we're all okay."

"I knew you three were trying to trap the jenny, so when I heard the shot, I thought maybe a mountain lion had made trouble," Zane said.

"They were attacked by an ATV driver," Jude said.

Zane stared. "Why would anybody do that?"

"That's what I'm here to find out," Jude said. "See any trespassers on your property?"

"No, sir, but I was talking online with a friend, so I wasn't exactly on high alert."

"Any trouble with ATV'ers before?" Jude asked.

"Couple months ago I had some ATV'ers down by the river. I told 'em the land's protected and they left peaceably enough. Sorry I didn't get any names."

"Going to cover the area now," Jude said. "Permission to search your property as well?"

"Of course. Whatever you need to do. Oh, I should tell you my dog Barney is missing. He's a champion hunting dog with a bad attitude. He might be somewhere on the property, but I can't find him. Had to put his buddy Fred down and I think he's upset about it. Probably won't bite, but he's a barker for sure."

"Thanks for the heads-up." Jude reached for the radio clipped to his shoulder.

Zane turned again to Felicia. "I've been having a laugh looking through our old yearbook like you suggested. Can't believe we were ever so young. It's like looking at somebody else's life."

Nora silently agreed. High school was a lifetime ago.

Jude spoke into his radio before he turned his attention back to them. "We'll take it from here and I'll contact you all with follow-up questions and arrange to return your truck and trailer when we can."

"And there's a drone too," Seth said, giving Jude the location. "I'd love to get that back."

Jude nodded. "We'll probably be here for a few hours, Zane."

"Yes, sir. Whatever you need to do is fine with me." He said goodbye and put a foot into the stirrup. "We aren't open for tours right now. Had to close for some cleanup work, so no one has any business being on the farm property, especially not at this hour."

"Good to know. Call the station if you think of anything else."

Zane nodded and swung up on his horse. "Take care of yourself, Felicia. I'll call you tomorrow."

They both smiled and Felicia waved until he was out of sight.

"I'll drive you ladies home now, if you'd like," Seth said.

"Thank you." Nora climbed into the rear seat. She felt like crawling into the smallest hole she could find. Felicia got into the passenger side. "Zane and I are going to touch base tomorrow," she said. "I'll see if he can give us any helpful intel on catching the jenny."

The donkey had eluded capture and that meant Nora was stuck in Furnace Falls. Not only was it a place that held all her deepest shame, but now there was a violent ATV driver added to the mix. Catching that donkey couldn't come soon enough, Nora thought as the red lights of Jude's car strobed the night.

THREE

Seth drove to the Rocking Horse Ranch, mind whirling. After they dropped Felicia at her mother's modest home outside of Furnace Falls, a ponderous silence descended. Seth was never comfortable with long silences, which worked fine since Levi Duke, his best friend and co-owner of the ranch, would happily listen for hours to Seth's ramblings with barely a comment. At least he'd gotten Nora to climb into the front seat so he didn't feel like her chauffeur. Turning on the radio didn't do much to smooth over the awkward quiet. Just before they rumbled onto the ranch property, she spoke, startling him.

"I'm sorry."

He darted a look at her. "'Bout what?"

"Everything, but mostly implying you were a coward."

"It's okay."

"No, it's not." Nora stared out the window.

"You could have stayed with your drone and called the cops, but you charged in to help two women you've never even met in person. I was frustrated and rude. I'm…not careful about what I say. My mouth is my worst enemy."

She looked so downcast, he urgently wanted to ease her discomfort. "But you're great with M's."

Her delicate brows crimped in puzzlement. "What?"

"M's. After my head injury, I had the worst trouble saying words with M's for some reason. Doc said I had to retrain my mouth muscles, so I spent hours blowing bubbles, chewing gum, whistling. Drove people to distraction. Took me forever to get the M's back."

"Must have been frustrating," she said.

"Yep." He let out a little chuckle. "Particularly since my sister's name is Mara."

Her responding laughter lingered in his ear like music and he looked over at her. In the dashboard lights he could properly see her heart-shaped face and the mouth that he suspected could be sweet and generous if she allowed it to be. Funny how a laugh could change a person completely.

They drove onto the property, and he pointed out the features of the ranch he co-owned with Levi; the main house where Levi and Seth's sister Mara, newly married, lived, the shack he occupied, which he'd nicknamed Castle Castillo, the distant corrals that housed the ranch's two dozen horses. He'd spent his formative years in Furnace Falls, fallen in love with the wide open spaces before he'd joined the army with Levi fresh out of high school, but the dream had always been to return and start a life of ranching. And he had, never imagining his sister would fall in love and marry Levi and come to live there too. He'd made the small shack his own after his sister married, and he enjoyed the cramped space. Why wouldn't he when he was surrounded by Levi's Duke cousins, Jude, Austin and his wife Pilar, Willow and her husband Tony, Beckett Duke and his wife Laney. An enormous black dog raced from the main house, barking.

Seth rolled down his window. "Banjo, sit," he yelled over the chaos.

The dog did not sit, but he stopped barking, slopped a tongue over Seth's hand before accepting an ear rub. "Banjo's more bark than bite," he told Nora. "Considering his best buds are a cat and a three-legged jackrabbit, I guess he's not your typical dog. Come to think of it, nothing on this ranch is typical. Most of the horses were rescues and castaways until Levi collected them."

Banjo rerouted to the passenger side and Nora reached out a tentative hand, which the dog licked extensively.

The door of the main house opened. Levi strode to the Bronco. His hair was neatly trimmed, and the knee of his jeans was patched.

Levi nodded when Seth introduced Nora. "I remember you from high school."

Nora stiffened. Seth noted that Levi refrained from adding that he and Jude had become as close as cousins could be over the years. Levi never said anything unless he had to.

"Thank you for letting me stay," Nora said.

Levi shrugged. "It's Seth's ranch too. Shout if you need anything."

Seth nodded as Levi returned to the house.

Nora had fallen again into a silence that continued as he opened the door of the old Vintage Cruiser trailer. He snapped on the light, hoping the smell of varnish had dissipated.

She climbed inside. "Wow," she said. "Not what I expected."

It didn't sound like a total compliment. "My pet project."

She took in the paneled walls, the padded seats around the tiny kitchen table. "You did a great job with the renovations. It's wonderful. Very retro."

Retro? He blinked. Should he focus on that

or the "wonderful"? "Yes, I guess it is." He hadn't ever thought of it that way. He'd simply been bent on recreating elements of his grandparents' trailer. And in his mind his work wasn't finished, probably would never be. He would still be tinkering with the place for years. "I'll fix you something to eat while you change."

"You don't need to do that."

"No trouble. I didn't eat dinner either." After a moment's hesitation, she went into the cramped bedroom and closed the door. Wondering why he felt a hum of pleasure at being able to feed her, he jogged to the main house and grabbed some ingredients, then returned to the trailer.

She came out of the bedroom wearing jeans and a soft blue T-shirt that mirrored the azure in her eyes. Her hair was still damp but curling into a fringe around her cheeks. He heated a pan and cooked a few eggs, managing not to burn them, then slid them between slices of sourdough bread with cheese for a quick sandwich.

They sat together at the small table bookended by the padded seats he'd painstakingly reupholstered in a cheerful blue. He launched into grace and got to the "amen" before he realized her lip was between her teeth and her brows were drawn.

"Not a believer?"

"It's complicated," she said, the words as taut as a pulled bowstring.

He took up his sandwich, noticing the shadows of fatigue smudging her face. There'd been more than one sleepless night for Nora. The woman before him was burdened, no doubt. Who wouldn't be? Especially after a close call on her life? But this went deeper, he sensed.

She ate a mouthful without seeming to taste it. "I've been trying to imagine why anyone would want to run us down. We weren't trespassing. We had permission from Zane and we weren't even on private property when we were attacked."

"Some person driving around who figured on a little malicious entertainment?"

Her frown told him she didn't buy the theory. He didn't either. "Possibly a drug deal going down that we interrupted? Some other criminal situation that someone didn't want us to witness?" he suggested.

The whine of an engine filtered in from the outside. Nora dropped her napkin and her eyes went to the door.

He put a hand on hers. "Probably nothing. I'll check." But as he went to the window he couldn't think why someone would be approaching the ranch at such a late hour. Banjo was in the house with Levi and the rain had masked the noise of the arrival, so there had been no canine alarm. He pulled the curtain aside and Nora peered over his shoulder, her hair tickling his neck. A man got off a motorcycle and Seth relaxed. "It's Doc Parson. I forgot to call him."

He opened the door. "In here, Doc."

The paunchy vet cut Seth a surprised look and trudged to the trailer porch. Seth introduced Nora and invited him in, but he declined. "Muddy boots. I've been out delivering a calf. Thought I was supposed to check on a donkey for you."

"There was a complication," Seth said. "We didn't get her."

Doc guffawed. "That jenny outwitted you, huh?"

"Not exactly." Seth told him a few details of the attack.

Doc's smile vanished and he scrubbed a palm over his thinning hair, eyes wide. "At Zane's place? Can't believe that."

"I wouldn't either unless I'd been there," Nora said.

"Some trespasser, I guess." He huffed out a breath. "You gonna go back for the jenny?"

"Tomorrow," Nora said.

Doc frowned. "Maybe not worth it though.

Might want to let it go and try again in a couple of months."

Nora shook her head. "I don't want this donkey wandering around for that long. She doesn't look well to me and she could get into trouble. We'll get her tomorrow."

He nodded. "All right. Call me when you want that exam." He straddled his motorcycle which had a little cargo trailer hitched to the back, kicked it to life, and drove away with a backward wave.

They went inside and finished their meal. Seth tried to keep the conversation going, but she was clearly deep in thought. When there seemed nothing else to say or do, he bid her good-night. "I'll be in Castle Castillo and I can see your door from there. Text me if you need anything."

"I can't. I dropped my phone somewhere."

"Oh. Well, flick the porch light."

"Won't you be asleep?"

"I don't sleep much."

She smiled. "We're a match, then." She seemed to regret the comment. "I mean, I don't sleep well either."

"Ranch air is good for sleeping, so they tell me, and if it means anything, you're surrounded by nothing but wide-open acres of peace and quiet."

She shivered. Maybe wide-open acres weren't real soothing when she'd almost been killed in similar topography. He wanted to touch her, to reassure her that she was not alone. Instead he shoved his hands in his pockets and smiled.

"Good night, Nora."

"Good night."

He was almost to the door when his phone buzzed. "It's a message from Jude for us," he said as he read the screen. "They found the ATV."

She was at his side in a moment. "Where? Did they get the driver?"

"No, it was at the bottom of a gully, so it took a while for them to locate it." He frowned as another message appeared. "They found something inside though. He's texting me a photo." The tiny image appeared and he thumbed it open. It was a photo of a torn piece of paper with a smudge of dirt across it. The paper was a printout of a screenshot. As they looked, he heard Nora's breath catch.

"It's from the Big Valley web page," Nora murmured. The shot captured a picture of Nora and Felicia posing with a rescued burro.

"The attacker had our pictures," Nora said. Her eyes locked on his.

He reached out to touch her arm, felt her

tension as the significance bore down on both of them.

The ATV attack was not random.

Felicia and Nora were targets.

And whoever had done it was still out there somewhere.

Nora felt every one of the nighttime hours pass by in slow motion. The small room in the trailer was perfectly comfortable, charming even with its glossy wood cabinetry and vintage refrigerator. A porcelain bowl painted with holly and snowflakes was on the counter, filled with peppermints. Snagging one, she sniffed it, but the mintiness didn't appeal so she stuck it in her jacket pocket. She hadn't noticed before but there was a silver Christmas tree in the corner encircled by a train track. She'd had nothing to do with Christmas trees since she'd left home, except for the tabletop version in their apartment that Felicia insisted on.

She bent to see the miniature train paused in its progress around the track. The vignette was nostalgic and homey, but none of it felt right. She was supposed to be on her way back to Colorado with a rescued donkey, resuming her regularly scheduled life. Instead she was pacing the new floor of a trailer in her old hometown, wondering who'd tried to kill her and Felicia.

She'd been convinced it was a random attack, but that theory had gone out the window when she'd seen that the ATV driver had pulled their pictures from the internet. She crawled out of bed, wishing she could text Felicia. The loss of her cell made her feel even more vulnerable.

When the thoughts whirled out of control, she stepped out onto the porch and breathed in the desert air, crisp, clean, pure. The sky was showing the first streaks of silver threading through the ebony but the winter stars were still visible now that the rain had stopped. That was the thing that had always amazed her. No matter where she was in the world, she knew the wide glittering constellations were somewhere overhead, but only in Death Valley could she see them so clearly. A dull pain thumped in her rib cage. What if she'd done things differently in her teenage years? What if she had believed her mother instead of her father? Would she have stayed in Furnace Falls, made a life under this starlit canopy? Would she still have a connection to God?

"What-if" played like a monotonous drumbeat until she walked to the pasture fence in an effort to change the rhythm. The soft whinny of horses and the scrape of a pitchfork told her someone was already at work, probably Levi, since she heard Banjo's excited bark. She tried to let the peace of this idyllic spot permeate her cells. The day ahead would bring stress starting at her 9:00 a.m. appointment at the sheriff's office with Jude.

A soft clearing of the throat made her spin on her heel.

Seth stood with two steaming cups of coffee. "Sorry I startled you. Levi handles the predawn chores, but I couldn't sleep and I saw you from the kitchen. Coffee?"

She accepted the mug. "Thank you."

"My pleasure." They sipped as they watched the sun ease its way into the sky, injecting streams of yellow and then orange into the horizon.

"My family lived in Furnace Falls for a while, but I moved away after the army," he said after a while. "Didn't ever know Jude very well, but I never heard him mention a sister before."

"I'm one of those siblings people would rather not introduce into polite conversation."

"Hard to believe."

She looked at him. "Why?"

He shrugged. "Kin is a big thing here, like it is in most small towns. Levi and his twin sister Willow are tight with their cousins Beckett and Austin Duke. Matter of fact, Willow's then-fiancé was in trouble not three months ago and the Dukes rallied around and sent a killer to jail." He blinked, as if his eyes had gone moist. "They also helped rescue my little sister Corinne. The Dukes all live in Furnace Falls, a stone's throw from each other."

The message was clear. The Dukes were good people. How could she be any different? Nora drank a deep swallow of hot coffee. Normally, she'd tell off someone who was prying into her family situation, but for some reason, she didn't feel like doing so. Maybe because Seth was a biological outsider instead of a Duke. Perhaps there was a glimmer of a chance that he might understand. She took a breath. "My family busted up. It came out my freshman year that my father had done some bad things. I didn't believe it, not for years. Jude and I both chose different sides. He was loyal to Mom and I sided with my father."

He nodded. "That must have been hard."

"I didn't handle the whole thing well. I could say it was my age—I was only sixteen when the whole mess started—but that doesn't matter in the long run. In my late high school days, I, uh, acted out in a number of ways and by the time I was eighteen—" She swallowed, hard.

"The bottom line was Felicia lost her dance scholarship because of me."

"She must not blame you too much. You two are like peas in a pod."

"Her mother does."

"Did, maybe? That had to be ten years ago. Time does even things out, at least I hope so." He paused. "I was driving Mara to Furnace Falls last year to make preparations to move to this ranch when I was shot in the head through the front windshield. Ended up in a coma. My family thought I was a goner."

She jerked a look at him. "That's terrible."

"It was, but I survived, more or less intact so that's a win."

"Are you always a glass-half-full kinda guy?"

He laughed. "Not always, but God gave me another chance at life, and I'm not gonna waste a moment, if I can help it."

Nora turned away. Great. She was about to be proselytized to. If she just believed more, trusted the Lord, her burned bridges would suddenly be restored and life would be grand and rosy.

He didn't say anything further, to her surprise. They drank their coffee, accepted a quick greeting from Levi and Banjo, who was followed by a crystal-eyed cat.

"That's Tiny. They're best buddies," Seth explained. "They don't seem to know they're not the same species."

She bent to stroke the petite kitty and the dog who shoved his head in for some attention.

Seth's phone buzzed and he pulled it out, flipping it to speakerphone.

"Good morning, you two," Felicia said. "Hope you got more shut-eye than I did."

"Probably not," Nora admitted, noticing a patch of stubble Seth had missed during his morning shave. He had a strong chin. She'd always admired a man with a strong chin.

Felicia sighed. "After Jude's revelation, my mother is demanding I stay inside closed doors all day, but I told her I have to go to the police station and we have a donkey to catch. Zane called to tell me the jenny is still on the property. He's delaying putting out the feed until we get there. Should be able to corral her pretty easily."

Nora exhaled in relief. She'd been afraid Felicia would be too scared to follow through on the capture.

"We're on to her wily ways," Seth said. "And this time, there will be no ATV attack."

We? Nora took in his genial smile, the reddened scar near his brow from his injury. She didn't want to encourage this "we" idea, but thinking about what had happened the previous night took her pride down a notch. The truth was there was somebody in town who wanted her or her friend, or both of them, dead, and they might have succeeded if Seth hadn't intervened. She made up her mind to capture the donkey and leave Furnace Falls immediately. Whatever trauma had occurred could stay buried here with all the others.

"I'll meet you at the police station. Nora, I, uh, sort of promised Mom I'd stay until after New Years." Felicia rushed on. "Seems like the least I can do after all the worry I've caused her and it will give me time to catch up with Zane. Can you handle getting the jenny to Colorado by yourself?"

Nora's spirit plummeted but she kept her tone cheerful. "Sure, no problem at all."

They said goodbye and finished their coffee. She declined Seth's offer of breakfast. He was doing too much for her already.

At the sheriff's office, the desk clerk led them into a shabby conference room that smelled of burnt coffee. A ragged tinsel wreath was pinned to the wall as a nod to the holiday. Nora ignored the clerk's curious glances. She was probably a hot topic of office conversation…the prodigal sister. *Get your money's worth, because I'll be gone by tomorrow.*

Without Felicia. The thought caused a pang in her heart.

As much as she tried to maintain an aura of calm, her stomach was clenched tight by the time Jude strolled in. He dumped a stack of files on his desk and took a seat. "Morning." He pushed a box across his desktop. "The truck and trailer are still on the bridge, but it's cleared for you to take. Here's the drone and your cell phone, Sadie."

She started to speak when he held up a palm. "Sorry, I mean Nora."

She took the phone without answering. Had he said it with derision or respect? It pained her that they had grown so far apart that she couldn't read him anymore. He was a proper adult now. Gone was the playful boyishness she remembered, covered over by a mask of cynicism.

"We've gone over the crime scene and done our cursory checks of you and Felicia," Jude said without preamble. "And we've got nothing that sheds any light on who would be targeting either of you."

He waited.

And so did she.

Seth looked from one to the other. "I'm no cop, but could it have something to do with the donkey rescue? It's the common factor, right? Both women work there."

Nora frowned. "Felicia and I started working there ten years ago when her friend got us a job mucking stables. We moved our way up from there."

Jude's dark blue eyes roved Nora's face. "Have you made enemies in the course of your rescue work?"

Again, she felt uncertain about his tone. Was there an undercurrent of challenge? "Not around here."

"Elsewhere?"

"I've reported property owners for animal neglect and abuse. Some of them haven't responded well, especially when they were fined and threatened with jail time."

"It's possible we're looking at a local. Makes sense since the attacker knew where to steal an ATV. I spoke to Felicia's mom about it. The driver took it from her neighbor's yard, but neither of them had a clue who might have done it." Jude began to click his pen again.

For the second time, she and Seth went over the series of events and Jude added notes to a yellow pad. At least it stopped him from the maddening clicking of his pen.

"Felicia's staying in town for a while, she tells me." Jude quirked a brow. "How about you? Maybe returning to Colorado would be safest."

"Donkey first, then home," Nora said firmly.

"We're going to try again on the donkey after we leave," Seth volunteered. "But if there's a threat to Nora and Felicia, might it follow them back to Colorado?"

"I've already reached out to the local PD in Ouray, so they're aware. They have no more ideas about motive than I have. Neither does your donkey rescue director."

Nora blinked. "You contacted my boss?"

His gaze was flat. "Doing my job."

And counting the minutes until I leave town? She forced herself to stare at the tough-eyed cop but found no traces of the brother she'd known. "I'm going to stay here until I can do mine."

"My best advice is to go home." Jude paused. "That's not a personal agenda item, by the way."

"Really?" She held her chin up.

Again he gave her the flat, emotionless stare. "I'm not the gatekeeper of this town. If you want to spend the holiday here, no one's stopping you. Just watch your back." He added, "And one personal favor." His mouth twitched. "Don't hurt Mom any more than you already have."

Nora's face went molten. A list of retorts scrolled through her thoughts but only one made it out of her mouth. "I was too young to have to choose, Jude."

And there was the barest ripple of emotion in Jude's eyes, as if a pebble had been thrown into a pond, but it was gone as quickly as it had arisen. "You've had a decade to grow up, haven't you?"

She felt the arrow cut through her heart. Seth put a hand gently on Nora's shoulder. Her first instinct was to shrug it off, but she didn't.

"Doesn't seem like anyone should have to pick between a mom and a dad," Seth said quietly.

Jude's eyes never left Nora's. "In this case, the choice was clear. Our dad was a cheater and a gambling addict. In spite of a mountain of facts and my mother's patient explanations over the years, Nora refused to believe that. She chose *wrong*." There was no veneer of politeness covering these words.

Seth started to speak but Nora cut through his reply. "I know that now, but at the time I was a kid. And what if I had changed over the past decade, Jude? Would you have welcomed me back? Listened to an apology? Offered one yourself?" Hating herself for the wobble in her voice, she walked out.

Seth fell in behind her, carrying the drone.

Nora tried to steady her erratic breathing. *Keep moving.*

At the main door, Felicia and her mother were talking. Olivia Tennison looked much the same to Nora, down to the ponytail of silvery hair, neat blouse and trousers. She ran a delivery business in and around Death Valley, Nora recalled.

"Hey, guys. How'd it go?" Felicia asked. "We finished up our interview but Mom stopped to talk to the desk clerk."

Nora shrugged, still too shaky to answer.

Felicia looked at her more closely but did not press. "I'll see you at Zane's in an hour or so. Mom's loaning me the Range Rover so you don't have to pick me up."

Olivia pushed past Nora without a word of greeting, but the scowl that pinched her face said it all. She and Felicia left. Nora stopped for a drink of water at the fountain, to give herself a moment. The cool sip didn't help calm her nerves.

A moment later, they emerged into the parking lot. Nora stalked to Seth's vehicle, her mind whirling.

Nothing was forgiven where Olivia was concerned.

And nothing with Jude either.

This wasn't her home anymore. There was

only unforgiveness here, and now an unidentified threat. *Do your job and get out,* she told herself, *before anything else goes wrong.*

An envelope was wedged in the frame of the passenger window. Distracted, she picked it up. It was heavy for its size.

"Nora?" Seth said, a step behind her.

"What's this?" she said, waving it at him.

His eyes went round with terror. "Don't move," he said.

Terrified, she froze, staring at the letter that she now realized was not a letter at all.

Seth eased the envelope out of Nora's fingers and walked as steadily as he could away from Nora and the building. "Get Jude," he instructed over his shoulder.

Nora ran inside and returned a moment later with Jude.

Jude pushed Nora back toward the station wall, eyes riveted on Seth. "Bomb squad's on its way, but it will be a while. Can you put it down?"

Seth did, lowering it millimeter by excruciating millimeter onto the pavement. Sweat poured down his face until finally he eased it to the ground and backed away.

Nora stood, her bottom lip caught between her teeth, trembling. When Seth joined them, he reached a hand to her. She took it, holding on to his strong fingers as if he would otherwise float away, or maybe she would. "How… how did you know that was a bomb?"

He smiled grimly. "Heavy envelope, grease stains, bump where the trigger is hidden inside. Military service makes you savvy." He paused. "And the fact that someone recently threatened your life."

Nora's grip tightened before she let go and hugged herself. He knew what she was thinking and he wondered too.

Why did someone want her dead?

FOUR

Nora tried to get her fear under control as they drove away from the sheriff's office. If Seth hadn't stopped her from opening that letter… She glanced at his profile. He'd risked his own life for hers. Again. She would not have thought such a lion heart was concealed behind an easygoing, self-deprecating demeanor. *Stop staring,* she told herself.

"Are you okay, Nora?"

She rallied a brave tone over the clamoring in her stomach. "Well, I didn't open a letter bomb, thanks to you, so I guess that's a win."

He covered her hand with his own. The gesture startled her.

"That was terrible…and the conversation with your brother wasn't fun either."

His touch was as warm as his tone, but she didn't dare discuss the matter that was clawing at her heart. "Past baggage between us," she said with a shrug that enabled her to move her hand from his. "It's what I expected."

"Expected, but it still hurt, right?"

She shrugged and looked out the window. Why did she feel like sharing with Seth? Not like he could do anything about it. Instead she blew out a breath. "Thank you again. If you hadn't stopped me from opening that…" She couldn't bear to say the words. *She'd be dead.*

He nodded. "Happy I was there."

She couldn't imagine why he would be pleased to be in the line of fire for someone he didn't even really know. *Just being nice*, she thought as they took the turn to the date farm.

"You know, if you don't feel up to this, I can—"

"I'm fine," she said, a little too sternly. "I mean, I'm ready to capture this donkey." *And get out of Furnace Falls.*

Felicia and Zane met them at the bridge where the truck and trailer were still parked. Nora got out. The morning chill lingered and for some reason she felt it more deeply today than usual. Uneasily, she scoured the brushy areas on the perimeter of the farm.

She didn't miss the rifle slung over Zane's shoulder as he joined them. Seth filled them in quickly on the letter bomb.

Felicia's paled. "Oh no. I cannot believe it."

"Nothing's gonna happen this time," Zane said. "Not on my property." He wrapped an arm around her shoulders and squeezed.

Felicia offered a brave smile. "Zane and I figured out a plan. He'll put out the feed as soon as we give the go-ahead. Nora, you drive the truck to the corral. When the jenny's in, there are boards we can use to guide her to the trailer. Hopefully, she won't freak out."

"Too bad Levi was busy," Seth said. "He can calm down anything with hooves."

Zane nodded but his eyes roved the tree line.

"Expecting trouble?" Seth said.

Nora's heart lurched.

"Nah, not really. Just weird to me, the whole ATV thing. Can't figure out why anyone would target two women rescuing a donkey."

"Me neither," Felicia said with a shiver. "And then the letter bomb."

Zane took her hand, tentatively. "No problems today. I promise."

"Promises, promises," she teased. "You promised to take me to see the Eiffel Tower someday. I still have the little drawing you made."

He blushed to the roots of his dark blond hair and Nora laughed. "Felicia has a memory like an elephant," she said.

Zane quirked a grin. "Dunno if that's good or bad. I'll go lay out the food. A half a flake of hay and a couple of bananas, just to be sure. Doc told me when he was here last that he'd never met an equine that could resist a banana."

Seth sent up the drone. Within five minutes, he had a visual. "Feed is delivered," he said, "and donkey girl is on her way." He and Nora parked the truck and trailer near the corral. They got out, crouching low and moving quietly to the fence where Zane and Felicia joined them. When they came into view of the animal, Nora caught her breath. "Something's wrong with her."

Indeed, the donkey was painfully thin except for a bulging tummy.

"She's pregnant," Nora said after a gasp. "I don't know how we didn't see that in the video footage." Pregnant, but sick. Her coat was dull, thin in spots. Tawny gray on top and white on her swollen belly and legs.

Nora grabbed a pair of binoculars from her pack and zeroed in. "She's got nasal discharge and she's massively underweight. Maybe a respiratory infection." Worry laced her tone.

"We'll get Doc in as soon as we clear the property," Seth said.

They tiptoed closer. While Nora and Felicia crept into the corral, he quietly swung the gates partially closed, resting them against both sides of the open trailer, trapping the jenny. She turned her silvery muzzle to look at them but didn't appear inclined to move. The banana she'd taken between her teeth dropped to the ground and she didn't try to retrieve it.

"That's not a good sign." Nora readied a rope and they all grabbed the boards. Donkeys were adept at kicking both to the rear and sides, and it was far easier to encourage them to move than to drag them where they didn't want to go. The donkey stood still until Seth and Nora closed in from behind, urging her toward the trailer utilizing the cover from their boards. The donkey remained motionless until the board gently touched her hindquarters. Without so much as a kick, the jenny allowed herself to be ushered through the corral and up the ramp Felicia had laid out to the trailer. Nora's frown deepened as she secured the rear doors. She turned to Seth. "Can you—"

"Already messaged the doc," he said. "We can stop by his office on our way to the ranch and maybe he can do an initial exam right away."

Her shoulders relaxed a notch. "Thank you."

"Gotta earn my keep."

She chuckled. "I owe you, remember? I'll buy you lunch."

"Excellent. I will be sure to collect on that offer."

She felt a tingle of pleasure at the thought of spending time with Seth. She was wondering what to do about her strange feelings when Zane rejoined them.

"Donkey rescue complete," Zane said. "But she doesn't look good. My brother Kai was more the horseman than I ever was, but I know enough to see that."

Felicia frowned at the mention of Kai.

"But you've got two horses," Seth teased. "How do you manage them?"

"Some of the guys who work the dates for me are horse owners." Zane's body straightened, his focus suddenly riveted on a cluster of trees on the road above them.

Seth went still. "What is it?"

"I thought I saw something," Zane said, shaking his head. "Maybe I imagined it."

Felicia grabbed Nora's forearm. "Not again. An ATV?"

"No," Zane said. "A glint, sort of like…"

"Binocular lenses?" Seth finished.

They exchanged a look. Something as innocuous as a glint of light could mean the situation was about to explode. She was sure he knew it; he'd lived it during his time in the military. He urged both women to the truck as Zane jogged toward the bushes.

Nora finished securing the donkey, climbed into the driver's seat, with Felicia next to her, her eyes wide with fear.

"Turn on the engine, but stay put," Seth said. He didn't want them driving into another ambush. "Call Jude if anything develops."

"What are you going to do?" Nora asked.

"Back up Zane."

Nora handed him the rifle from the back of her truck. Her mouth was drawn into a tight line of determination. She wasn't going to let herself or her friend—or her new rescue—fall victim to an attacker the second time.

"No need," he said with a comical wink. "I'm a lethal weapon without a gun."

Nora watched him turn, sprint then skid to a stop when Zane reappeared on the path, shoulders slumped. His frown said it all as they returned to the women.

"Didn't see anyone?" Nora asked.

Zane held up a pair of binoculars. "No, but I found these."

Chill bumps rose on her arms as she recognized them. High-powered binoculars, like the kind hunters or military people used. The glint of glass had indeed been a clue that they were being tracked. Someone was still out there. Watching.

And waiting.

Zane offered to remain on the farm to wait for Jude. Felicia insisted on staying with him, over Nora's objections.

"We'll hole up in the farm office with the doors locked until Jude arrives," Zane had promised. "I won't let anything happen to Felicia." His forehead was furrowed. Seth could imagine his feelings. Someone was sneaking around the guy's property again, and for the second time they hadn't come close to catching him or her.

Nora and Seth waited until the two had entered the small wood-sided office that also served as a store. The porch pillars were twined with colorful Christmas lights that seemed at odds with the frightening episode they'd just experienced. When the two were safely inside, Seth tried not to tailgate as he followed Nora's truck and trailer off the property.

They passed under the elegant date palms, bare of fruits, over the bridge where Nora had tried to ambush the ATV driver, and away from the farm. Seth scanned the terrain as he trailed her. It felt like the clouded desert sky cast deeper shadows than normal, offering plenty of concealment for Binocular Guy. Would there be another attack out of nowhere? Normally he'd accuse himself of paranoia borne of having been shot in similar terrain, but at the moment all he could think about was that Nora was a potential target. And how close she'd come to opening a letter rigged to explode. Why, he simply couldn't imagine, but that wasn't the important fact. Seeing her safely off the property was his number-one mission.

His mission? Kind of presumptuous since she didn't want him around. He straightened in the seat. She might not want a connection between them but, like it or not, she was getting his guard services until she was safely on her way back to Colorado.

When exactly had he decided that? he wondered. Probably while witnessing that painful interaction with Jude; the moment he'd gotten a glimpse of the wounded Nora, her heartbreak at a past she couldn't undo. He knew what that felt like, and he wouldn't wish it on anyone. When his fiancé Tanya dumped him, it had felt like a body blow. Somehow, he'd discerned Nora's heart was soft and tender and she needed an ally whether she realized it or not.

As Seth jogged away, he tried to decipher what he'd seen on her face when the avalanche of memories had stopped him from accepting the gun. Had she believed him a coward for not taking it? Why did it matter so much what she thought of him?

As they traveled between two boulder piles, he tensed, looking upward for any signs of falling rock. There were plenty of places where Binocular Guy could shove a massive pile of granite down on them. Sweat slicked his hands as they crept by. He hadn't realized he was holding his breath until they were clear and rolling onto the highway.

With each mile, he relaxed a fraction. By the time they arrived at Doc's tiny stucco-covered veterinary office, his pulse had almost returned to normal. Doc's wife, Renee, was behind the desk with a phone to her ear. Her long rust-colored hair trailed down to her shoulders and she shoved it back, setting her jingle bell earrings tinkling as she gestured them in. Covering the receiver, she whispered, "I haven't been able to get hold of him yet, but he should be back any minute. Have a seat, okay?"

They settled into uncomfortable plastic chairs. Doc and his wife had attempted some holiday cheer with tinsel garland along the reception desk and felt stockings taped to the wall, but the decorations couldn't overshadow the cracked and yellowing paint and the gouged squares of linoleum. Doc's practice wasn't exactly thriving by the looks of things.

Renee toyed with a strand of hair with the hand that wasn't holding the phone. The outer door opened a few minutes later and Doc strolled in. Seth and Nora stood.

Doc squinted at them. "I didn't expect you here," he said, looking from his wife to the visitors. From somewhere in the back, a dog started in on a mournful howl.

"I messaged you," Renee said to her husband. "You really should learn to check your phone once in a while."

Doc smiled tightly. "Right. I forget about that technological umbilical cord. Thing runs out of charge constantly." He turned back to Seth. "Give me one minute, would you?" He disappeared down the hallway.

Seth offered Nora a reassuring smile. "Doc's the best, but he's always behind schedule since he takes way too much time with each client."

Nora nodded, frowning. Her thoughts were clearly with the struggling donkey. Better there than considering the stalker lurking in the woods, he figured.

Doc returned five minutes later, the howling ceased. "Got an office buddy who freaks out whenever he hears my voice. Couple of moments of attention and a chew bone did the trick. Did you get the jenny this time?"

"Yes," Nora said. "She's in the trailer out back. She needs immediate attention."

He grabbed his medical bag and followed them outside, where Doc started on his exam, leaning through the window openings with his stethoscope to reach her. The donkey shifted uneasily but did not kick up a fuss. He used a hypodermic to extract a blood sample, then took her temperature. "She's got a fever, an ulceration on her eye, obvious malnutrition, and nasal and eye discharge."

Nora blew out a breath. "Infection?"

"Undoubtedly. Where'd you catch her?"

Seth relayed the events.

"Zane helped you out, huh?" Something in the doctor's tone caught Seth's interest.

"Yes. He found a pair of binoculars too. Someone out there watching the proceedings."

Doc froze, one hand holding the syringe filled with the donkey's blood. "Yeah? Why would anyone do that?"

"I don't know. Do you?"

Doc looked at Seth before he turned his attention to the animal. "Someone interested in Zane's business? How do I know? Humans make way less sense to me than animals."

"That's for sure," Nora said. Had she caught

the vet's momentary hesitation also? But her attention was fixed on the suffering donkey as Doc climbed down from the trailer.

"I'll get this to the lab, but we'll treat her right away regardless. She's a sick one, for sure. Bacterial infection most likely, which we can address with antibiotics. The bigger problem is that she's extremely malnourished and ready to give birth. We've got to get her strengthened or she won't survive that. Might not anyway, to be clear."

"I understand," Nora said. "I want to give her the best chance. Tell me what to do."

"While we treat the infection, we'll have to start her on a refeeding program and give her a vitamin/mineral block, limited grazing time away from other animals if she's strong enough, and some vitamin and fluid support. I'd say she's days away from giving birth, so we don't have much time."

Nora looked confused. "Oh, she can't stay in Furnace Falls. I have to take her back to the sanctuary in Colorado right away. Just give her what she needs for the journey."

"To Colorado?" He shook his head. "I wouldn't advise it until after she's given birth."

"But we've got experts there—" Nora started then stopped. "I didn't mean…"

"Experts unlike a small-town vet?" Doc's

eyes narrowed then he offered a tired smile. "I've raised everything from dogs to donkeys since I was three years old. You're welcome to leave with her, but I don't think she'll be alive when you get to Colorado. Let me know what you decide." He gave the listless donkey a shot and a quick pat on the side. "You'll be all right, little lady," he murmured to the animal.

Nora turned a tortured look to Seth. Her struggle was clear. She desperately wanted to leave Furnace Falls. But would she do it at the expense of the animal?

"I could take care of her," he said quietly. "With Levi and Doc's help. Keep you in-formed, if you need to go back."

Nora cocked her head at him before she slowly shook it. "No. She's my responsibility, and you and Levi have other things to tend to. I'll figure it out." She turned to Doc. "Thank you. I'll keep her here until after she foals. I know you'll give her great care and I'm sorry if I offended you."

Doc cradled his medical bag like a football. Though his face was tired, his grin looked genuine. "Long as you pay your bills, all is forgiven."

Nora returned the smile. Seth marveled at how the grin changed her face, like the shift from winter to springtime. "The sanctuary is paying the bills, but I'll take care of the labor," she said.

Seth glanced at Nora. "So you're staying at the Rocking Horse then?"

Her smile was replaced by a wince of discomfort. "I…uh…"

He made sure his own expression stayed casual. "The trailer is yours for as long as you need it." And she would need to be close to the ailing donkey. With Christmas a little more than a week away causing a run on the hotel rooms, the trailer was the most practical answer. But she might feel indebted to him, or the Dukes, and her pride might not allow that.

Doc went inside, leaving them alone.

"I know you don't want to stay here in town," Seth said. "You've got good reasons, a messy past and someone stalking you. I'm not pressuring. The trailer is empty if you need it, but I completely get it if you decide to go elsewhere."

She folded her arms across her chest. "I'd rather eat nails than stay here."

He had to chuckle. That pretty much said it all.

"I'm sorry," she hurried to say. "I didn't mean…"

He raised his palms and laughed. "No offense taken." But he felt his spirit drop. Having her there on the ranch gave him energy, an excitement he hadn't felt since long before his injury, prior even to his fiancée's abandonment.

Her gaze wandered to the jenny. "But I'm not going to let some stranger or my own mistakes get in the way of taking care of this animal."

He straightened. "A determined woman."

She sighed. "My father used to say the best way out is always through. For all his faults, at least he taught me that." She raised her chin and looked at him. "I would be grateful to use your trailer, and Big Valley will cover the costs."

"No need. It's unoccupied anyway."

"They'll pay," she said firmly. He understood. She didn't want charity.

"All right," he said, extending his left hand because he never had to worry about it tremoring. "Right now we start on Mission Rescue Bubbles, headquartered at the Rocking Horse."

Returning his smile, she made his heart trip. "Bubbles? How'd you decide on that name?"

Seth grinned. "I have a nephew who's ecstatic for bubbles and, not to brag, but we blow gigantic ones. Our efforts to catch them are legendary. Name seems appropriate for a donkey that refuses to be caught."

As they were climbing into the trailer, Levi's sister Willow appeared, strawberry hair twisted into a messy ponytail and that smile she perpetually wore now that she was married.

She greeted them. "Hi, Seth. I thought that was you. I was on my way to get an ice cream."

He feigned shock. "At ten thirty in the morning?"

"It's got milk, and I need a break from staring at photos. My photography studio walls can start to close in on me sometimes." She looked curiously at Nora. "Why do I feel like we know each other?"

That was Willow. Always direct. A blush stained Nora's cheeks. "I…think we had some classes together in high school." Then she took a breath and offered her hand. "Nora Duke, but you probably knew me as Sadie."

"You're Jude's sister?" Willow said, gaping. "Wow. I haven't seen you in years." She pulled a frown. "Levi told me someone was staying in the trailer but, of course, he didn't bother to explain it was Jude's sister." She rolled her eyes. "My brother never offers up extra syllables unless he's required to."

Nora offered a tight smile. "It's confusing."

"I remember you now." There was a moment of silence and Seth knew Willow was probably recalling the accident details and Nora's abrupt departure from town. She recovered quickly. "Anyhoo, since you're staying on the ranch, just a heads-up we're having the Duke tree trimming tonight. Our cousin Beckett's barbecuing an absolute mountain of meat because he says no one else can do it right." She paused. "You're invited."

"Oh, I…uh, I'm sure that's a family thing. Besides, I have paperwork to do."

Willow blew out a dismissive breath. "Your last name's Duke, right? So you're family. You belong here if you want to," Willow said. Before Nora could reply, she said goodbye and hustled away.

Nora was silent as they got into the truck.

"I…" she started and then stopped. "I'm not sure it's a good idea for me to stay on the ranch."

On instinct, he reached out and clasped her fingers. "You don't have to do anything family related if you don't want to. But if you do, I promise it will be okay."

She considered, chewing her lower lip. "The donkey will foal soon and, with some treatments, she'll be able to be moved. This is a short-term thing."

She seemed to be telling herself more than him. He didn't interrupt.

As long as she would stay in the trailer, he could be sure Binocular Guy, whom he was pretty sure was ATV Guy and Letter Bomb Guy, wouldn't get anywhere close. And he sure wouldn't mind the excuse to get to know Nora Duke better.

FIVE

Nora decided the only approach to handle the painful situation was to take it a day at a time. She'd have to find a way to stay on the Rocking Horse Ranch and take care of Bubbles that didn't cause Levi or Seth any extra work, and certainly without attending any family functions. Regardless, she'd probably be working closely with Seth. The very thought made her nerves go all fluttery. *Don't you have enough to worry about without focusing on Seth?*

She texted Felicia to let her know the results of Doc's exam. Levi was at the ranch to supervise the unloading of the donkey into a fenced paddock that housed a miniature barn. It was neatly painted a rusty red color.

"We have rescue horses pretty regularly," Seth explained, "so this is their quarantine accommodation until they can be acclimated. It'll be perfect for Bubbles."

She had to agree. Bubbles would be secure,

warm and comfortable at night when the temperatures dropped, but she'd also be able to see people and horses coming and going, an important first step in domesticating her...if she survived. The donkey was still way too listless and it pained Nora so see the ribs protruding against her dull hide. Levi leaned his elbows on the rail and watched.

Seth described what Doc had recommended. "He said she might not make it."

Levi nodded. "We'll see. She can get to know Floyd if she sticks around."

"Floyd's a donkey Levi rescued from a neglectful owner. He's a character," Seth explained then he turned to Levi. "We have other problems you should know."

Levi listened, mouth quirked to show his surprise as Seth told him about the letter bomb and the binoculars. "The guy's after you and Felicia then?" he said to Nora.

"Looks that way." She paused. "If you aren't comfortable with me staying here, I understand."

Levi shrugged. "Between myself, and all the Dukes coming and going, this is the safest place in Furnace Falls. And Willow's the best shot of all of us, save Jude." He paused. "Willow's already called to tell me to count you in for the party tonight."

"Oh." Nora could not push out an answer through her suddenly dry mouth, but Levi didn't seem to notice. Without another word, he waved and strode back to the main house.

She didn't want to delve into a conversation with her emotions hopping like fleas, but as if he knew that, Seth merely guided her to the far end of the paddock, let her through the gate so she could examine the stable. Everything inside was perfectly in order, from the fresh bedding to the full water trough and small amount of hay and loose salt. It calmed Nora. At least if the outcome was bad, the jenny would be comfortable and safe for her last days.

Nora stepped out of the stable into the paddock. The jenny eyed her. Nora moved closer one small step at a time until the donkey's ears flattened.

"I'm here to help. We're going to get you through this. You're going to get well and have your baby and we'll find a home for you," Nora said. Home was what this jenny needed the most. A home where she felt secure, confident that she would be cared for unceasingly. Who didn't want that?

Nora recalled her mother and brother standing shoulder to shoulder in the doorway after high school graduation when she'd left her family and Furnace Falls for good. She hadn't looked back, in spite of her mother's sniffled cries. Nora wouldn't have wanted them to see that she'd been crying too. That teenage Nora had been a confused young woman who could not accept a truth that had devastated her a few hours before, the truth about the man she'd idolized, whose chin dimple she'd inherited, along with a passion for donkeys.

Bubbles took an unexpected step and shoved her nose forward. In a flash, she'd swiped the peppermint from Nora's pocket and danced away before she slicked it out of the wrapper and swallowed it. Nora laughed.

"Got ourselves a pickpocket," Seth called, laughing.

It was a good sign, she thought as she backed away and exited the paddock just as her phone rang.

"Hey, Nora," Felicia said. "How's our girl?"

Nora gave her a quick report. "Touch and go, I'd say, but she's got an appetite for candy."

"She'll make it." Nora caught a distracted tone in her normally ebullient friend.

"What's wrong? Aside from the obvious."

"Nothing, probably." Again an uncharacteristic hesitation. "I'm at Zane's and he's on the phone. Let me step outside." Nora heard a door close. "Zane's very upset by everything, of course. I think…" She trailed off.

"You think what?"

"Do you remember Zane's brother, Kai?"

The question surprised her. She mentally scanned her high school memories. "Actually, I do. I think I only met him once. He was a year older but I think he repeated a term, right? He went to a different school eventually, didn't he?"

"Yeah, the kind they send you to when you steal cars and beat people up."

This was getting serious. Nora looked at Seth. "Mind if I put this on speaker for Seth?"

Felicia agreed and recapped.

"What happened to this brother Kai?" Seth said.

"Zane didn't want to talk much about it. I get the sense Kai left the area and came back only for their mom's funeral. When the date farm went to Zane, Kai took his part of the settlement and left. I gather it wasn't a cheerful parting. Zane said his brother had problems, but he wouldn't be more specific."

"Are you thinking that Kai is behind the ATV attacks and the binocular thing?" Seth said.

There was a long pause. "I don't know. What would be the purpose? If he was angry at Zane, why attack us? I'm gonna look through my old stuff and see if I can jog my memory about Kai."

"And we'll ask Jude to check on it," Seth said.

Felicia breathed out. "Weird."

"Felicia," Nora said, "is there something you're not saying?"

She hesitated. "I'm sitting on the porch, alone, but I feel like someone's watching me."

"All right," Nora said. "You need to leave there immediately. If Kai's on the property…"

"Don't worry. I poked my head in and waved goodbye to Zane and I'm walking to my car now. I'll text Zane later." They heard the sound of the car door shut and the engine come to life.

"Stay on the phone with us until you get to the main road," Seth said.

"Okay. I'm going to Mom's. I promised to help put up the Christmas decorations today and be there for dinner. Nora, can you come over tomorrow morning so we can talk?"

Nora's mouth went dry. "Your mom doesn't want me around, Felicia."

"Text me and I'll meet you on the porch. We can go get coffee or something. I'll use the Range Rover instead of the truck so you don't have to detach the trailer or anything."

"All right. I'll come at nine, after I feed Bubbles."

Felicia agreed, let them know she'd reached the highway, and they disconnected.

Seth glanced at her. "Not my business, certainly, but what happened when you two were in high school?"

Her gut reaction was to clamp her teeth together and remain mute. Instead she found herself telling Seth the truth.

"My dad, um, he betrayed our family and I didn't believe my mom and Jude about it. First heard about it when I was sixteen and it started a downward spiral for me. I went kind of wild, walked away from my faith, and family, started to go to parties. Felicia and I went to a party our senior year and I drank too much." She felt the pain of it again, the raw shame wash over her. "I drove us into the side of a feed store, ruining Felicia's knee, which resulted in the loss of her ballet scholarship. When the legal trouble and the financial dust had settled, we hatched a plan to start over again. We ran away from home on graduation night after I... Well, I discovered proof positive that my father was exactly who Jude said he was."

"Ah. I think I understand a little better now." Seth walked her to the trailer. "For what it's worth, I admire you for staying here now."

She looked at him in surprise. "You admire *me*?"

"Uh-huh. You've got plenty of reasons to speed out of Furnace Falls, but you're here, even though it makes you uncomfortable. That's courage, pressing in instead of running away."

She couldn't explain why tears crowded her vision at that moment. "Thank you. I…don't think I would be able to if you hadn't been so kind."

"Like Willow said, you belong here if you want to."

She fell into the comfort of his words for a moment, allowing the fantasy of a home and family to enter her brain, fill it with cozy images, before she brushed it away. Home and family didn't belong in her reality.

"I don't want to," she said, hoping it did not sound rude. "I need to be very clear about that, Seth. I'm here for the jenny, then I'm leaving." Why did she feel it necessary to state the obvious? Was she saying it for him or herself?

He held her gaze for a long second and she thought he might have looked regretful. Suddenly, she wanted to take back the words, rest her head on his chest and let his heartbeat ease away her angst. Silliness, she chided herself. Nothing but emotional fallout from the traumatic day.

But it was too late. At her words, he said he'd see her later and went to tend to his ranch chores.

Nora let herself into the trailer. "Home away from home," she said with a sigh. This time it did not feel quite as strange. She helped herself to a few crackers from the box Seth had brought over. It had been nonstop stress since she'd returned to town and she felt depleted down to her bones.

Her gaze found the series of photos on the opposite walls of Seth's carefully restored trailer. He'd wanted to remake the space to honor his grandparents, but the photo gallery captured memories from the Duke clan as well. She drew close, fingers tracing one filigreed frame. It showed Kitty, her mother, her arm crooked through Jude's as he escorted her to a seat in a church. Jude was dressed in a suit and Kitty in a fluttery dress of lavender, her favorite shade. Her face tipped sideways, away from the camera, a longstanding family joke that she never liked to have her photo taken. Seth was there too, leaning on a cane. Her mother looked small next to Jude, her head barely level with his shoulder, diminished somehow. How much Nora had missed in the ten years she'd been away.

She flashed back to her days as a grade-schooler when she and her teen brother Jude had pretended to be wilderness scouts, scouring every tiny patch of water for the endangered pupfish that only lived in precisely two miniscule habitats on the entire planet. Never mind the impossibility of their hunt, Jude was always willing to indulge his baby sister and they'd skulk around for hours.

Her memories flipped back to one of their blowups.

"You just want to make me hate Dad because you hate him," she'd screamed at her mother, an angry sixteen-year-old.

"I don't hate him," her mother had said, finally raising her voice to a shout, hands clenched into fists. "I want you to see him for what he is."

"He didn't cheat on you, he wouldn't," she'd spat.

Jude had arrived home from his police cadet work then, flinging the door open in time to hear her.

"He did," Jude thundered, "and he spent all your college money on gambling and his new girlfriend. Dad isn't the hero you make him out to be. Why don't you wise up and take a look at the truth?" Jude's eyes had blazed in a way that made him unrecognizable as the brother she'd grown up with.

"That's not true, Jude. Tell him he's out of line, Mom."

But her mother had looked at the floor.

At the time, Nora couldn't imagine why the two wanted her to believe such terrible lies about Ron Duke. The accusations about the man she'd worshipped could not be true. He'd attended every one of her softball games and tasted each of her disastrous home economics recipes for school. She was his "mini me" he'd always said. Her mother and her brother might betray Ron Duke, but Nora never would.

And she hadn't. The betrayal had come from his end, when she'd learned a few years later on her graduation night with 100 percent certainty that Jude and her mother had been right.

Turning away from the photo, she pulled out her laptop and wrenched it open. Might as well get her work done. It would give her an excuse for not attending the party or wallowing in self-pity.

The emails were quickly finished and she found herself looking up Kai Freeman. There wasn't much to be found on him online, so either he was using another name or he stayed away from social media.

Was it possible Zane's troubled brother was behind the ATV attack and the binocular incident? But, like Felicia had said, what would be his motive? What would he gain?

And why would he want Nora dead?

SIX

Seth relished the mellow Death Valley temperatures as he completed his part of the endless ranch chores. It was the air in the desert that made the region so unique, he'd finally concluded. Or maybe the quality of the sunlight that rendered everything in its truest colors. Whatever the reason, a perfect morning in Furnace Falls never failed to cheer him, for a few moments anyway. Levi was still doing the lion's share of the horse handling, because Seth had not yet recovered full strength in his right hand and arm. That was maddening. At what point exactly would he be able to convince Levi he was the same man he'd been? Maybe the problem was convincing himself.

Wrong approach, he thought. He wasn't the same man and never would be. Mostly that was a good thing, God had made him realize. Now he knew deep in his bones that each and every day was a gift. Sure, he'd realized that to some degree before, especially in his army tours, but now it was set in cement, buried deep. That truth flavored his soul and gave him a ravenous appetite for life.

Resolutely, he thanked God that he was present and able to clean out the stables and be there to help Nora with Bubbles and watch over her. His thoughts seemed to drift to Nora as if tugged by a persistent wind. Her strength was what made him marvel, her willingness to stay here and stand her ground though she had to feel ill will piling up around her like dunes of sand. The family wreck, the anonymous assailant, Olivia's blame. He wondered what he could do to ease her stress. And why he desperately wanted to.

There were so many captivating things about Nora. He liked that she was tall, close to his six feet. He liked that her eyes were the rich blue of a storm-darkened sky. He appreciated that she was smart, savvy and spoke her mind with enough humility to apologize when needed. He admired how she loved wayward, unattractive donkeys when she could have dedicated herself to more perfect specimens. To his surprise and trepidation, he realized he'd come to like Nora Duke very much indeed in the few months they'd known each other, a process accelerated when their Zoom visits had turned into face-to-face time.

Take it easy, buster. She said she'd rather eat nails than have anything to do with Furnace Falls and that includes you.

Duly admonished, he let work occupy him until late afternoon when the Duke family arrived, including his sister Corinne and her young son Peter.

The women beelined into the house, probably to admire the newest batch of outfits they'd purchased for Laney and Beckett's sweet-natured baby Fiona, all pink frilly stuff. Or maybe to consult about the new computerized booking system for the ranch used to schedule horseback riding expeditions. You never knew with those whip-smart women.

Beckett tied on his "King of the 'Cue" apron and got to work at the outdoor grill, his black beard highlighted against the white smoke. The Duke couples settled into chatter and business.

Seth was the proverbial third wheel, the jovial uncle. He was grateful, deeply grateful, yet he wondered if God would ever provide him a life partner. Longing crept in when he surveyed the cozy family tableau.

The men got to work erecting the wooden tables, two long ones set end-to-end for the family, another that would hold the holiday feast.

"When's the tree coming?" Seth got his answer when a pickup pulled up, driven by Jude, who tapped the horn. A pair of felt antlers and a red nose had been wired to the grill. In the bed lay a pine tree so robust it overlapped the bed. Jude parked the rig.

"That tree is ridiculously huge," Levi said. "What were you thinking?"

"Go big or go home. We got little tykes now and that changes everything, right?" Jude said as they helped him lug the tree out and secure it to a wooden platform in front of the house. They set about putting on the strings of lights.

Seth's sister Corinne peered out the window, watching her six-year-old son Peter as he exited the house and made his way to his uncle, stopping to look up at the massive tree with wonder in his eyes. Seth gave Corinne a thumbs-up. He understood why she was fearful of letting the boy out of her sight after what she'd been through.

"Hey, Big Man," Seth said.

"Hi, Uncle Seth." Peter turned to wave to Corinne as if to reassure her he was fine.

"Corinne looks so happy you're here for your first Duke Christmas tree trimming," Seth said.

They hadn't yet progressed to the child calling Corinne "mommy" since he'd been raised by another woman his whole life. They'd get there, he figured. Corinne was mature well beyond her years, he thought proudly.

Peter tipped his head and Seth took a knee, which brought them into a closer visual range. "Auntie Willow said there's a donkey. Can I see it?"

"Right this way," Seth said. "We'll be back," he called to the other men who were still wrangling long strings of lights onto the enormous boughs. Jude waved distractedly at him, frowning over the spaghetti tangle of wires.

Better you than me, Seth thought with a grin.

At the corral, he found Nora, again approaching the donkey and talking softly to her. She held out a hand, not touching the animal, who raised her nostrils to sample the air. After a long moment, Nora took one step closer before retreating.

"What's she doing?" Peter whispered.

"Showing the donkey that she doesn't mean any harm. Bubbles is a wild donkey, so she needs to learn to be around people."

"Oh," Peter whispered again. "Corinne says it's scary to be around people sometimes, like I felt when I started first grade."

Seth's heart twanged and he touched his nephew's shoulder. "You're brave, just like our Bubbles here. She's going to have a baby soon, a foal."

"Cool. I can't wait."

"Progress?" Seth asked when Nora joined them.

"I think she ate some and her eyes look better to me." After Seth introduced her to his nephew, she said, "Hi, I'm Nora."

Peter solemnly extended a hand and they shook. "When is that donkey gonna have the baby?"

"Very soon," Nora said.

"Like tonight?"

She laughed. "I guess we'll find out."

"Corinne says there's a donkey in the Jesus story." They spent a good half hour watching the donkeys, listening to Peter's chatter. Finally, Peter looked back toward the house. "They're going to light up the tree." He jogged away and stopped. "We gotta hurry. Come on."

Peter stood there, gesturing for them both to follow.

Nora jammed her hands in her jacket pockets and retreated a step.

"Don'tcha want to see the world's most enormous ranch Christmas tree?" Seth said softly.

Nora's mouth twisted. "I…"

He didn't press.

Peter called again. "Hurry, it's almost time."

Sensing Nora's resolve weakening, Seth offered a crooked arm. "Just a look. No obligation to socialize. Personally, I enjoy watching Jude and Levi try to boss each other around about tree-lighting methodology."

After a long hesitation, she took his arm for a few steps, which sent a thrill clear to his shoulder. As they approached the gathering, she let go. The scent of pine infused the air and the women had come out of the house. They introduced themselves to Nora. Jude was still fiddling with the light strings, which was probably a relief to her.

Peter hopped up and down with excitement as Levi picked up the extension cord.

"Ready?" Levi called.

"Ready!" was the shouted reply.

Levi fitted the plug in the outlet and the giant tree blazed to life with what seemed like a million colored lights.

"Awesome!" Peter hollered.

Little Fiona squirmed in her mother's arms, reaching her hands toward the sparkling sight. "I think Muffin wants to help decorate," Laney said.

Beckett had come over and kissed his wife and buzzed a raspberry onto the baby's cheek, which made her laugh. "We got way too many ornaments, as usual, so she's welcome to help, but first, we gotta eat the chicken because it's ready."

"Bossy," Jude said.

"Yeah, he is." Willow transferred bowls of salad and baked beans to the table, which was now covered with holiday-plaid linens and set with dishes and cutlery. "All stern and no suave, just like Jude."

"Whatever," Beckett said placidly. "It's chicken time."

Seth noticed Nora edging back.

Jude caught Seth's eye. The cheerful demeanor had vanished, replaced by a grave expression. Gone was the jovial civilian, back was the cop. It was eerie how he could switch gears so quickly. He pantomimed that he needed to talk to them both.

The nerves tightened Seth's stomach. Nora shot him a startled glance.

"Probably just a follow-up question or two," Seth said.

Nora looked as though she might sprint off. He walked away from the tables toward Jude, wondering if she would follow. Jude and Nora were as wary as the wild donkey, their lack of trust putting miles between them.

But family drama would have to wait. There was still the matter of an unresolved hidden threat.

Someone wanted to hurt Nora and Felicia, and they had to find answers. Before it was too late.

* * *

Though her legs screamed at her to get away quickly, Nora found herself trailing after Seth. She burned to know what was going on with the case.

Jude wasted no time getting down to business. "I need a word with you both first," he said. "I thought I'd update you with what I got on Kai Freeman."

Nora forced herself to keep looking at him even though she felt like his gaze went right through her. "I'm listening."

Jude took a moment to rally his thoughts. "Kai is a year older than Zane, but he had to repeat tenth grade for truancy reasons. Then, because of his expulsion, he completed his senior year at another school."

"Why'd he get expelled?" Seth asked.

"A classmate made fun of his car, an old Mustang he'd been restoring. Kai waited for him after school and assaulted him. His attack put the kid in the hospital. It wasn't the first time he'd been in trouble for violence, so he was expelled. His mom sent him to a private school known for discipline, smaller student population, et cetera. It was a boarding school, so he wasn't in town except for holidays. After he graduated, he left and returned only for his mom's funeral that I can tell. He finished alternative high school and worked for a demolitions company for a while in Reno after graduation. He was fired for insubordination. After that, the trail gets foggy. He lived briefly at a hotel in Arizona while he worked construction jobs. Hasn't been seen here in town recently, at least not that I'm aware of." He paused. "That's not to say he couldn't be holing up somewhere close by. I asked Mom if she remembered anything about Kai, since she knew Zane's family somewhat."

Nora swallowed at the mention of her mother.

"Mom said Kai was easily bored, had trouble connecting to the other kids, but he loved his brother. It was hard for him when he was kicked out of public school and they were separated. Real painful for his mom because Kai nursed a lot of anger at her decision to send him away. Their dad died in a car accident when the boys were young, so it was all on her."

"You said he worked for a demolitions company," Nora said. "Do you figure he might be involved with the letter bomb? And what about the ATV attack? He knows the area well."

"I don't know. We haven't gotten any conclusive fingerprint matches from the letter bomb yet. And there were no usable fingerprints from the stolen ATV. There were a myriad of prints on the binoculars, including Zane's, which makes sense since we now know they were hanging in his barn where he and his workers used them occasionally. Suffice it to say we have no leads yet."

That wasn't at all what Nora wanted to hear. She'd survived two attempts on her life and whoever was behind them was still out there. Waiting to do it again?

The conversation died away as Corinne clanged a dinner bell.

"Going to eat with us?" Jude's words startled her.

"No. I just came to see the tree lighting."

"We'd love to have you," Seth hastened to say, "but if not, I'll pack up a plate and bring it to the trailer." He looked at Jude, brow creased. "You're okay with her staying though, right?"

There was a challenge in Seth's tone and Nora felt herself flush. Why did Seth feel as though he needed to butt into her business with her brother? She didn't require a champion or a defender. She simply wanted to get out of this place. While she was trying to decide on a reply, Jude answered.

"Fine with me either way," he said.

She doubted that.

Nora felt caught in the spotlight but how

could she get away without being rude? Corinne made eye contact and patted the chair next to her, and Nora found herself slinking into the seat and bowing her head while Seth said a simple prayer of thanksgiving for the season and the company gathered there.

Nora felt more trapped than thankful.

When she looked up again, Jude was watching her.

Professional interest probably, but at least his expression was neutral, not hostile.

Somehow, she made it through the meal, which was delicious. It was interesting listening to the ebb and flow of easy conversation and teasing amongst the Duke clan who obviously cared about each other. But she wasted no time excusing herself from the table when dinner was done.

Seth walked her to the trailer.

"Enjoy your dinner?"

"Yes," she said. "I didn't expect to, but I did."

"All the Dukes and their attached are good people." He opened the trailer door for her. "Still meeting Felicia tomorrow?"

She nodded.

"How about I give you a ride?"

"No need. I can take the truck."

He looked disappointed but stepped aside

so she could enter the trailer. "I, uh, well, my former fiancée Tanya used to say I am one hundred percent involved when fifty would do. Feel free to tell me to back off."

Former fiancée? She had no idea the unassuming Seth had been engaged. She wanted to ask him about it but didn't want to pry or upset him. She turned away and looked back across the property at the family captured in the glow of the outdoor lanterns. It was such a warm, tender scene, and it touched a nerve deep inside her. Seth was a part of that loving circle and for some reason he appeared bent on helping her. And she found that she welcomed the notion, to be near his cheerful spirit, the genial smile, the genuine caring in his heart for those around him. An enticingly attractive package. She instantly put an end to those thoughts. *He's a friend, a good friend. Nothing more.* So, she reasoned, what could it hurt to accept a ride? "Actually, Seth, I'd be grateful for the lift."

He gave her a goofy thumbs-up. "All right. Coffee and breakfast are always ready in the kitchen at eight o'clock. Sleep well, Nora."

She locked the door behind him. Snatches of laughter drifted through the air as the dinner cleanup continued. Looking up at the trailer ceiling, she thought about her earlier years when she'd have thanked God for her blessings.

Don't get confused. Whatever you had here in Furnace Falls is gone. That's not your family out there and Seth is only a temporary fixture in your life. Pain settled under her ribs as she rolled onto her side and closed her eyes.

The text from Felicia startled her.

Glad you're coming tomorrow. Found something that makes me worry.

Nora sat up. Her fingers were slightly shaky as they typed.

What? Do you want me to come now?

Tired. Show you in the morning. Love you.

Love you too, Nora typed. She tossed and turned, wondering what Felicia's troubling revelation might be.

After her sunrise chores with Bubbles, Nora caught the acrid smell of burned food when she was still yards from the main house. Inside, Seth was trying to fan away the lingering smoke.

"Whoa," she said. "Burned the eggs?"

"To cinders. I got distracted. Levi decided skipping breakfast was better than a blackened scramble, so he left. I was going to try another batch."

Nora took the pan from him without a word and produced a pan of fluffy eggs. "My mom is a great cook. She taught me well."

"Thank goodness," Seth said. "Or we might've had to eat leftover baked beans for breakfast."

They ate in relative silence, chatting only about Bubbles and donkey care and Levi's hydroponic garden in the corner, bristling with greens. It was pleasant to be in Seth's company and enjoy a meal together, in spite of her worries. Two in the space of twelve hours? The knowledge gave her the shivers. She got up to clean the dishes and he joined her.

"Too bad Levi gave up. He could have eaten your eggs."

"Snooze and lose, right?" *Keeping things light*, she thought.

He laughed. "Words to live by."

The question tumbled out of her mouth before she could second-guess it. "You mentioned a former fiancée last night. What happened with you two?" She began wiping a plate, aghast at her own curiosity.

"You mean why'd we break up?"

She nodded, her cheeks fiery.

"I think maybe I wasn't exciting enough. I loved doing things with Tanya and for her, everything from planting flowers in her window boxes to building a shelf for her photos. Then one day I noticed the shelf was pretty crowded with work photos and such, and not too many of us. She…developed feelings for her boss and gave me the heave-ho."

"I'm sorry," she said. "That must have hurt."

"Yeah, but it was four years ago. I'm a different person now and I'm sure she is too."

Nora could only hope Tanya had wised up. Tossing away a good man like Seth. Not that she herself had any ideas about him. After all, she was leaving Furnace Falls in her rearview as soon as possible.

"Ready to go meet Felicia?" Seth said.

"Yes. She's found something disturbing."

"What about?"

"I don't know. She wants to show me."

Dishes done, they hustled to the truck. Soon they were pulling off the main road and down a wooded lane to an old ranch-style home. Nora's fingers were knotted together.

"I haven't been here since we ran away at eighteen," she said. "Felicia's mom heard my car that night when I picked her up. She ran out, screaming at us not to leave." She blinked. "Bad memories."

"That's rough," he said.

She lifted a shoulder. "I'm glad she's rebuilding a relationship with her mom." Had she kept the wistfulness out of her voice?

The morning was cool, with a thick overhanging blanket of clouds. He stopped under a twisted elm and Nora texted Felicia. A moment later, the door opened and Felicia hurried out, a backpack slung over one shoulder, keys in her hand. And no smile on her customarily cheerful face. Nora felt a chill that had nothing to do with the weather. Whatever Felicia wanted to show her was obviously upsetting her. Or frightening her.

Phone in hand, Nora got out. "Thanks for the ride, Seth."

"Anytime."

"If you need a lift back…"

"Felicia can drop me off." She realized she'd sounded too brusque. "Thank you, though. You're very sweet." Sweet, and taking up far too much of Nora's headspace.

She thought he looked a bit crestfallen. "I hear that a lot." He shrugged. "Anyway, see you later."

She hurried to meet Felicia.

"What's wrong?"

"I figured something out, but I'm not sure I'm right. It's too weird. Let's go get coffee. I'll tell you on the way."

As Felicia rushed ahead and reached for the door handle on the Range Rover, Nora stumbled on a pothole and dropped her phone. As she bent to retrieve it, in her peripheral vision she saw Seth fling open the door of his Bronco.

"Stop!" he shouted.

She gasped as he sprinted toward them.

What on earth…? Her mind did not compute the danger until she saw the glint of a metal container underneath the Rover, positioned under the driver's side.

"Felicia!" she screamed.

But it was too late.

There was a deafening boom. An invisible blast of pressure assaulted her. As Nora flew backward, she saw Felicia lifted into the air, arms flung outward in a desperate reach before everything went black.

SEVEN

Seth stumbled back at the force of the explosion. Heat seared his face. He fought to regain momentum. Vision blurred and eyes stinging, he pressed on through a swirl of smoke toward the burning car. *Nora. Felicia.* He flashed back to his service years. Images of all the carnage he'd seen assaulted him; the men and women he had not been able to save.

Not this time.

He reached Nora first. She was crumpled on her side. Strands of blood-dampened hair darkened her forehead. Putting his cheek close to her mouth, he felt for breathing. What if... The words echoed through his veins until he shut them down. Medics could not afford those thoughts and, right now, that was his job. He replaced the what-if with "What do I need to do for her?" A faint warm stirring of precious air and the flutter of a pulse at her neck told him her heart and lungs were still functioning. A gush of gratitude left him breathless. She was alive and hanging on, at least for the moment.

He ran to Felicia next. She, too, had been blown off her feet, but she'd been at ground zero when the detonation occurred. The blast had left her blackened and bleeding, one arm extended, the other pinned underneath her. To his horror, he detected no breath, no pulse. He was reaching for his phone when the door of the house opened and Olivia ran out. She stopped so suddenly he could hear her shoes skid on the welcome mat. Frozen in shock, she stared at her fallen daughter.

"Call for help," Seth commanded, easing Felicia onto her back so he could start chest compressions.

Suddenly, Olivia sucked in a breath and began to wail, the shrill keening cutting through the desert morning. "No! Not my daughter!" She took a tottering step forward but Seth called out again, louder.

"Go back in the house and call for help now," he insisted.

His tone snapped her out of the panic. She closed her mouth and spun away. The call was probably redundant as the explosion had already brought two neighbors outside and they'd no doubt phoned for help. Never assume, he'd learned long ago. Better multiple callers than everyone figuring the others had done it.

Another car screeched to a stop and Zane got out, mouth slack, eyes wide. "What happened?"

Seth didn't know how Zane had arrived so quickly and right now he didn't care. "Make sure Nora is still breathing," he said. "Watch for the ambulance." From his peripheral vision, he saw Zane check Nora's wrist and breathing before he fetched a blanket from his car and tucked it around her. The neighbors arrived at a sprint, bringing another blanket.

"How's Felicia?" Zane called from Nora's side, but Seth had no extra energy to spend on conversation. Felicia could be moments from death. He'd experienced that same scenario more times than he cared to remember. As he performed CPR, he prayed he would see clues that she was reviving, but her body did not show any signs of recovery. After a full cycle of compressions, he stopped to check for a pulse.

"Come on," he muttered. "Don't give up, Felicia." His fingers found only still flesh with no flutter of a beat to give him hope.

Olivia ran from the house and fell to her knees at Seth's side, wailing so loudly Seth's ears rang. She pawed at his arm, mumbling incoherently.

The two neighbors stayed with Nora, and Zane came over. "Mrs. Tennison," he said, "it's gonna be okay. Seth was an army medic, Felicia told me. He knows what to do. He'll save her."

Don't make promises, Seth wanted to say. Felicia's survival was anything but certain.

Olivia didn't acknowledge Zane's comment. She grabbed Felicia's limp arm, sobbing.

"Mrs. Tennison." Seth tried between rescue breaths. "You've got to step back now."

Olivia ignored him too. Tears streamed from her unfocused eyes and she continued to moan and paw at Felicia.

Zane caught Seth's look and grasped her arm. "We have to let him help her, okay?" He half led, half dragged her away toward the two neighbors.

Relieved to have some distance between Felicia and her mother's terror, Seth timed his prayers to the steady rhythm of his actions. Compressions, breaths, pulse checks, repeat. In between, he called to the neighbor to get the first-aid kit from his truck and apply pressure to the deep wound on Felicia's neck and her damaged fingers. He continued without interruption. It seemed as though time slowed to a crawl, just as it'd done in combat situations when he'd waited with the fallen for transport. Finally, at long last, a neighbor said, "They're here."

Olivia's cries mixed with the sirens from the ambulance emergency vehicles. In his peripheral vision, Seth saw Jude run on scene with a firefighter and several medics, but his words faded into the background noise. All Seth could do was continue his efforts until the medics were in place. He turned to see that Nora was also receiving attention from another medic.

When the EMTs took over chest compressions and placed a valve bag over Felicia's mouth, Seth went to Nora and evaluated her as best he could while keeping out of the way. No obvious external bleeding, steady respirations. But he knew anything and everything could be going wrong inside. *Nora...why would someone do this to you and Felicia?*

He felt suddenly enraged, angrier than he'd ever been in his life.

Nora was loaded onto a stretcher with full spinal injury precautions and sped away. Felicia was transported a moment later. He knew the prognosis was dire. Car bombs were meant to maim and kill, and whoever had set this one intended just that.

One of the neighbors guided Olivia to an officer's squad car before they drove off to the hospital.

Zane stood with his hands jammed into his pockets. "She gonna make it?" he whispered.

Seth presumed he was talking about Felicia. "I don't know." His weak arm was shaking and his chest was tight with adrenaline and anger.

Jude's radio buzzed as he approached them, his face pale under his perpetual tan. Seth realized this was no impartial case, no matter what Jude wanted everyone to think. Nora was his sister and he'd just arrived to find her injured by an explosion. He wished Nora could see the emotion that Jude was trying hard to conceal at the moment. "You two okay?"

"Yes," Seth said. He hoped Jude would not press about his trembling arm. He did not need any pity.

Zane waved off Jude's concern. "I'm totally fine."

"What happened?" Jude demanded.

Seth tried to put it all in a concise report. He finished with, "It was a device under the car. Wish I'd seen it a moment sooner. Could have been wired to detonate when Felicia reached for the handle, or it might have been triggered remotely by a cell phone."

"Was it meant for Felicia or Nora?" Zane said. He'd wiped a smear of black across his chin. "Or maybe Olivia? It is her car." He groaned. "None of it makes sense to me. Stuff like this doesn't happen in Furnace Falls."

It does now. Seth's logical brain finally

wrested control from his frazzled nerves. "Why were you here, Zane?"

Zane blinked. "Me?"

"Yeah. You were on scene moments after the explosion."

Jude waited for the explanation along with Seth.

Zane's brow furrowed. "Are you implying I had something to do with this?"

"Not implying, he's asking." Jude said.

"You can see why I'd take offense," Zane snapped.

"And you can see why that doesn't matter," Seth snapped back. Jude sent him a startled glance. He breathed out and modulated his tone. "We're talking about a bomb, Zane. Anyone close could have done it." Seth handed his own phone to Jude. "You're not above questioning because you're a friend of Felicia's and neither am I."

Zane glared for a moment and then sighed. "You're right. I see how it looks, that I just happened to be Johnny-on-the-spot. Felicia and I had a phone conversation last night and she asked me to meet her here this morning." He held out his phone to Jude. "Do you want to see my call history? Or you can check for a detonation trigger on my phone if you want."

Jude took both phones and scrolled quickly

through both before he returned the devices. "I see the call that came in from Felicia's number. Why did she want to meet you?"

"I don't know."

Jude and Seth both stared at him.

He squirmed. "I mean, I might have a suspicion."

Jude stayed silent and it was all Seth could do not to shout, *Spill it, already.*

"She, uh, I think she believes my brother was behind the ATV attack. She asked me all kinds of questions about him."

Kai. It jibed with what Felicia shared on the phone earlier. The brother sent away to boarding school for bad behavior. Was he angry? Looking to ruin Zane's life?

"But you don't think Kai's responsible?" Jude pressed Zane. "Why not?"

Zane's gaze raked the crystal-blue sky. "I guess I don't want to."

"What does that mean?" Seth said.

Zane folded his arms across his chest, looking from Seth to Jude. "Would you want to believe the worst? If it was your sibling?"

Jude squared off with him. "I would want to make sure my kin didn't hurt anyone, if I had a way to stop it."

Zane shook his head. "This has to be a mistake. Kai isn't like that. He got into trouble, but there were always valid reasons. We were close. He went through a lot. My dad's death, anger problems. I know my brother and he's not a killer. And, anyway, why would he come back now and try to hurt Felicia or Nora? What'd be the point?"

It was a good question since both women had been gone from the area for a decade.

Jude was silent for a moment. "I don't know what Kai's motive would be. But there are a few indicators that someone could have been watching your place. The binoculars, the ATV attack. Likely it was someone who knew the terrain." Jude glanced at a firefighter hosing down the burning vehicle. "This car didn't explode itself and your brother worked for a demolition company, correct?"

Zane nodded, brow furrowed.

"When was the last time you saw him?" Jude asked.

"After my mother's funeral five years ago. The lawyer contacted us while we were staying at the farmhouse. It…surprised him that the farm was left to me. Surprised me, too, honestly. I thought it was all mortgaged to the hilt, but my mom had managed to right the ship." He shook his head. "Pretty amazing since she wasn't known for spectacular decision-making."

"So Kai was left out of the will?" Seth said. Substantial revenge motive.

"No, he got some money. A nice-size check."

"But he wanted the farm, maybe," Jude said.

"He didn't say. He left the next day and I haven't heard from him since." Zane sagged. "Look, maybe there's another enemy at work here. Hurting Nora and Felicia doesn't have anything to do with my property. And, like I said, my brother's not a bad guy. Certainly not a mad bomber."

Jude arched a brow. "Do you even know your brother anymore?"

The anger kindled to life again in Zane. "Probably about as well as you know your sister." He flung the taunt out.

The barb hit home. Seth saw Jude's expression harden to marble.

As much as Seth wanted to help nail whoever had planted the bomb, he ached to get to Nora. He could stand it no longer. "I'm leaving," he blurted.

Jude and Zane looked at him.

"I'll share anything I can later. Right now, I have to get to the hospital and see how they are."

Zane nodded, his gaze drifting to the smoldering car. "Me too. Felicia doesn't deserve this. I need to be there, no matter how things turn out." His Adam's apple bobbed as he swallowed.

No matter how things turn out... What would the news be when Seth arrived? Would he be told by a grim-faced doctor that he hadn't done enough? That Felicia and Nora hadn't made it? He thought of Nora's eyes, the courage that pulsed there.

Jude turned without another word and strode to his officers. Seth climbed into his truck, forcing his trembling hand to grip the wheel. In a fog, he drove to the hospital. Was Jude starting to believe that Kai might be responsible? But Zane had a point that outwardly the violence didn't seem to benefit anyone. On the way, he phoned his sister and she promised to alert the Dukes. Perhaps with their ears to the ground they might pick up a thread about what had happened. And they'd want to support Jude as he navigated the situation with his estranged sister.

His pulse still thrummed with a combination of anger and disbelief. He had to stop himself from running through the parking lot and into the waiting room area. It was decorated with fake holly and garish red Christmas bells that jarred his senses.

Olivia sat in a chair, her fingers twisted together. Fear aged her with shadows. A police officer occupied the seat next to her, gently asking questions and recording her answers in a notebook. Her grief struck Seth like a blow. He'd been there for what had to be the worst moment of her life, and he'd been unable to offer even a word of comfort. Sitting was impossible so he silently paced, waiting as others arrived. Zane was first, then Jude, then a lady with her flyaway hair clipped back who hobbled a bit as she entered on Levi's arm. Nora's mother, Kitty.

Olivia shot to her feet when she saw her. "What are you doing here? Get out. Your daughter is responsible for what happened."

Kitty recoiled and Jude stepped forward as if to protect her. "Nora didn't hurt Felicia, Mrs. Tennison."

Olivia's face shone with hatred. "She might as well have. She ruined Felicia's future back in high school. Her stupid choices took away my daughter's scholarship. Then she convinced Felicia to run away with her. Now she's gotten Felicia involved with something bad that might cost her life."

"I know you're upset…" Kitty started.

"Upset?" Olivia spat. "My daughter could die and it should have been yours that got blown up. Nora deserves it, not Felicia." Seth directed her away with his body while Jude shielded his mother from the verbal assault. The officer on duty hustled over, took Olivia firmly by the forearm and walked her to the far side of the waiting room.

"Thank you," Kitty whispered to Seth. Her face was ashen, her lips bloodless. "I didn't realize she hated my daughter so much."

"Grief and fear sometimes twist things," Seth offered. He, too, was surprised at the outburst. Her words kept reverberating in his mind, especially how she said it should have been Nora that got blown up. Exactly how did Olivia mean that?

"How…how are they?" Kitty said, breaking into his thoughts.

"Still waiting for word," Seth said gently.

As if on cue, the doctor appeared and introduced herself. She looked at the gathered group. "Family of Nora Duke?"

Jude and Kitty stepped forward. Jude gestured to Seth. "You're in this too."

Gratefully, Seth followed them to the corner where they settled Kitty into a chair. She wrapped her arms around herself as if expecting a blow. Jude gripped her shoulder.

"Your daughter is going to be okay," the doctor said. "Mild concussion and two bruised ribs. The scalp wound required a couple of stitches."

Goose bumps cascaded down his spine. She was going to be okay. Seth realized he'd been holding his breath.

Kitty reached out a trembling hand and Jude grabbed it. "Thank you," he said to the doctor. "What about Felicia?"

The doctor looked at them. "You're not family, I assume, but since you're the chief, I'll tell you it's touch and go. We're giving her all the support we can."

Seth's stomach clenched. He knew that kind of medical speak. Felicia's survival odds were slim.

From the corner of his eye, he saw Zane look at the floor. How must he feel that his high school love was gravely injured, possibly at the hands of his brother?

"Can we see Nora?" Jude asked.

The doctor nodded. "Keep the visit short and don't upset her. There's going to be plenty of psychological trauma to deal with in addition to the physical."

Especially if Felicia died.

After Jude and Kitty went in, Seth paced some more and spoke to his sister Mara and Levi when they arrived. They were both shocked and angered. Levi's arm was slung tight around Mara's shoulders as if he could keep the bad news from affecting her.

Mara looked close to tears, uncommon for his practical and unflappable sister. When Jude emerged with Kitty, Mara hugged her tight. "I'm so sorry, Aunt Kitty." Didn't matter that there was no direct bloodline, Kitty was an aunt to everyone. "Let us take you home, okay?"

Jude looked grateful as he kissed his mother on the cheek. "I'll check in with you later, Mom."

When they left, Zane walked over. "I heard Nora's okay. I'm so glad. And Felicia..." He gulped, paused and started again. "Can I see her?"

"No one except family sees her until she awakens and we can get a statement." Jude softened his tone. "I'm sorry, Zane, but I've got more questions. Can you meet me at the station in an hour?"

He shrugged. "Sure. I'm going to cooperate fully."

Jude watched Zane trudge away before he turned to Seth and extended a palm. "Thank you, for helping Felicia and my sister."

Seth returned the handshake, grateful that the tremor in his biceps had mostly stopped. "I hope it was enough. Do you think it's Kai?"

"I don't know, but I can promise you that the guilty person is going to pay."

Seth felt the same current of ferocity radiating through his own heart. Someone had almost killed Nora, and Felicia was still critical. It could just as easily have been Nora who was touch and go. The image of her lying hurt and helpless would forever be seared in his memory. Why did he feel like it was his duty to protect her? Part of that instant connection he'd felt from the first moment he'd "met" her on Zoom? There was something about Nora that nestled in his heart and made him think he couldn't live without her.

Get a grip, Seth. It's only post-traumatic stress.

Jude cleared his throat. "My sister didn't want us in her room. I can understand it, I guess. This isn't anyone's idea of a family reunion. I still don't agree with what she's done in the past, but I don't want her to be alone. She's distraught about Felicia, hurting physically. I cleared it with the doc so you could… I mean, if there's any way you can…"

"You don't need to ask, Jude." And it was true. Seth wanted nothing more at that moment than to be with Nora, to comfort her and, in doing so, comfort himself. He didn't understand the urge, but it was beating an undeniable rhythm inside him. "I'm going in right now."

Jude blew out a breath. "Thanks. I have to get back to the scene. I'll have a cop stationed here until she's released, and one posted at Felicia's room as well. After that, we'll restructure the security."

Security, he thought, landing hard back into reality. The boom of the explosion replayed in his mind… Nora and Felicia thrown to the ground like discarded rag dolls.

All his life he'd been the peacekeeper, a conflict resolver, but if someone tried to injure Nora again, they would face a kind of wrath they'd never known before. The unaccustomed anger rolled through him again. Puzzling.

With a final nod to Jude, he walked down the hallway toward Nora's room.

Nora felt herself drifting in a comfortable haze until her brain snatched her back.

Felicia. Terror chewed her nerves. Her memory coughed up only a frightening image of her friend pinwheeling backward and slamming into the ground before Nora's recollections were snuffed out by the force of the explosion. She knew Felicia's condition was grave by the way Jude had tiptoed around the issue.

"Where's Felicia? What happened to her? Please tell me." She'd practically begged him for answers when he'd come in her room before.

Jude had held up a soothing palm.

"Felicia's okay. She's on another floor. Let's focus on you."

Her? The empathy must be a byproduct of police training, but for a quick second he'd almost looked like the big brother she'd worshipped all those years ago. Had he been hiding a grimmer truth? Maybe Felicia was dead and he was reluctant to tell her. She couldn't separate her own confusion and the awkwardness of their forced reunion. Her brother was back in her life front and center, thanks to the explosion.

And her mother…

The woman was so much smaller than she remembered, more delicate and tremulous as she'd reached out to touch Nora's arm. When had her mother's fingers become slightly crooked, the joints swollen? Nora had wanted so badly in that moment to extend her own hand and meet her mother halfway, but she'd been paralyzed. Her mother's touch… What did it mean? How should she feel? The trauma and heartache were too much to bear. All she could do was clamp her lips together to keep from outright bawling as the pain assaulted her physically and mentally. Her body felt as though she'd been tumbled down a rocky slope, every tiny movement awakening a new ripple of discomfort. A headache slammed both temples in spite of the medicine the doctor had ordered. Even with her nerves blaring, she wanted to get out of bed and run to every room in the hospital, shrieking aloud until she found her friend. But what if she was not there to be found? Cold prickles erupted along her spine.

"Oh, God," she started. "Please…"

But her broken prayer only choked off in a swirl of panic. Why would He help her now when she had resolutely rejected Him after her flight from Furnace Falls? She didn't want Him anyway. She didn't want anyone. Her heart's desire was to wake up from this nightmare and flee to Colorado.

There was a soft knock at the door and Seth stuck his head in. Her emotions ran riot. As much as she told herself she didn't want connections with anyone in Furnace Falls, her spirit leapt to see him standing on the threshold. Sweet Seth, with his lopsided smile and bottle-green eyes. If she could have jumped out of bed and wrapped him in a hug, she would have.

Thank you, Seth, she wanted to say, *for your courage and compassion and for coming in here to check on me when I feel so completely alone*. Instead, she felt her insides go all to pieces and she began to cry big hot tears that she could not stop. Mortifying.

He moved to her and clasped her palms between his own, stroking gently and murmuring words she couldn't decipher. One of his hands trembled a little, not with emotion, she realized but the muscles acting out against his wishes. She'd seen it before, but hadn't remarked on it, knowing he wouldn't appreciate it. After a few moments, she realized he was praying. Prayer was the last thing she wanted from him or anybody.

"Don't…" she choked out, pulling away. "I don't need to pray."

He looked at her, the smile still warm and gentle. "No problem. I'll just slip outside to do it."

Always thinking of her feelings… Who was this man really and how had he become entwined in her world? It was disorienting. "No, I mean *I* don't, but if you want to pray, here's fine."

"Are you sure? The last thing I want to do is add to your discomfort right now."

She nodded. "I'm sure."

"All right." He handed her a tissue and bowed his head again. This time she didn't stop him. She listened as he poured out his fear, his uncertainty, and his obvious affection for her in a tender prayer.

Affection? How had that cropped up? Frighteningly, she felt the echoing fondness in her own heart. She wanted to stop him, but she found she could not. Instead she watched the crown of his curly hair, the way his generous lips moved as he prayed, the earnest entreaty in his voice; most of all, the calm that seemed to envelop him.

When he was finished, she realized some of his peace had overflowed to her. She hadn't felt that way since before her family had fractured and she'd chosen a side and taken that first step down a ruinous road. When he opened his eyes, they were the softer hue, like sunlight shining through new leaves.

"I stopped praying," she blurted.

"When?"

"After my father moved out when I was a freshman. I stayed with Jude and my mom until the end of high school, but it was terrible. She'd accused him of cheating and stealing my college money and gambling it away, but I couldn't believe it."

Why were the words pouring from her mouth? She didn't know, but she couldn't stop them. "On graduation day, I showed up at his apartment to invite him to come to the ceremony. His..." She stifled a cough. "His girlfriend answered the door. She wasn't much older than Jude. Their kitchen table was covered with betting sheets. It was laid out there, proof positive that my dad was everything I'd refused to believe."

"That had to hurt."

"Like nothing else. I felt like he'd died so I..." She considered. "I guess I figured if I'd lost my real dad I wasn't going to have a Heavenly one either."

He nodded. "That's painful, to lose them both." There was no judgment in his face, only empathy. It made her long to hug him close. *Stop this right now. You don't want Seth to get any closer than he already has. Stop talking.* She gulped and jammed a tissue to her eyes to keep him from seeing her inner confusion.

"Felicia," she said at last. "They won't tell me any details. How is she?"

"She's holding her own."

"Seth," she demanded, clutching the blankets. "I'm strong and I need you to tell me the truth. Is she really alive?"

The softness of his gaze did not completely hide an underlying gleam of steel.

"I would not lie to you, Nora. Felicia is alive. I promise you, she's in a room on the third floor, being taken care of right now."

She knew it was the truth. A great gush of

relief whooshed out of her. The news was all she could hope for. "Was it a bomb?"

"Looks that way."

"Like the letter. Who would do that? Kai?"

"That's what we're going to find out."

She shook her head. "All I want now is to make sure Felicia's will recover and take that donkey back to Colorado. Whoever the bomber is…" She shrugged. "Maybe we'll never know."

"Yes, we will," Seth said, a spark rippling across his face. "Jude's going to investigate and I'm going to help you tend to Bubbles and keep you safe until he finds out who did this."

The words were spoken softly but undergirded with iron.

"No, Seth. That's not your job."

Then he smiled. "Package deal. While you're on the ranch, you get a slightly banged-up ranch hand for an assistant. Didn't you know that?"

Emotion ballooned inside her. "Why?" she demanded. "Why am I your personal assignment?"

He was serious now, the teasing tone gone. "Because you need help."

Help. That was it. A pin pricked her swelling feelings and she deflated inside. She was a project. *Good*, she thought. *Now it's clear where I stand.* Seth was a good guy, but he wasn't her guy. Why had she conceived of anything else?

He grimaced. "I'm sorry. Did that sound—"

"No, I get it. Girl almost gets blown up. She obviously needs something."

"I didn't mean to imply that's the only reason I'm—"

She waved a hand and swallowed her pride. "I appreciate the help, even though I wish I didn't need it. But you're right. I do."

He still looked uncertain. "Tanya used to tell me I could write a book on all the wrong things to say." He shoved his hand under his leg and she realized he was trying to hide the tremor.

Now she looked closer and saw that his hair was darkened with smoke, and there was a slight spasm in his right leg as well. She'd been so busy focusing on herself, she hadn't considered that he'd dived into danger to save them. Empathy overrode her logic. "Were you hurt, Seth?"

"Nah," he said, jaunty. "My muscles just like to remind me that they are, in fact, the boss of me." They were back to the easy kidding rhythm.

The nurse came in. "I'm sorry. I need a few moments to care for Ms. Duke."

Seth excused himself and Nora felt a flutter of panic. Ridiculous. No one was going to sneak in and kill her. Were they?

"Are you leaving?" Had she really said that aloud? She was going to pieces now, surely.

"Nope," Seth said at the door. "Can't get rid of me that easily."

"Um, okay," she said, trying not to sound relieved.

The truth was, by the time the treatments were done, her nerves were screaming in pain and she was exhausted. She'd tried to pry information out of the nurse about Felicia's condition but she'd been every bit as tight-lipped as Jude. After the nurse, the police officer stationed at the door introduced his shift replacement and discussed the schedule with her. She listened intently, willing her headache away, as a plan formed in her mind. She had to see her friend.

When Seth returned, he was carrying a stalk of prickly purple thistles shoved in an empty water bottle.

She couldn't hold back a giggle. "You brought me thistles?"

"The gift shop was closed, but there's a nice patch of these babies in the lot outside which don't seem to know it's winter. The purple looks nice, right? I've seen donkeys chomp down these things like cotton candy, so I figure they must be awesome plants."

She looked again at the fluffy lavender puffs

surrounded by intricate rings of spines. They were kind of pretty, now that she took a close look.

"Remind me of you," he said quietly.

She blinked. "Weeds make you think of me?"

His face went dusky. "Not weeds." He gingerly fingered one of the blossoms. "A flower on the inside, surrounded by a serious protective layer."

She felt her own face glow, unsure whether she was happy or chagrined at the comparison. Seth made her feel off balance all the time.

He looked uncertain again, as if he was not sure he should have spoken his thoughts aloud. "Anyway," he said, settling into the chair, "you look tired. Why don't you get some rest and I'll hang out for a while to see if you need anything when you wake up?"

"All right," she said. She would not tell him about the plan she'd worked out. It could wait. For the moment, she was grateful that he'd be there watching over her while she slept. *Thank You*, she silently whispered, *for Seth*.

It wasn't really a prayer at all, she thought. She was not about to fall on her knees to the Lord or anything, but maybe it wouldn't hurt to express gratitude in a way that might help her process, like Seth had done.

When the pseudo prayer was complete, she refocused on the plan she'd concocted. She had to know, had to see Felicia for herself. She closed her eyes and waited for her moment.

EIGHT

Seth sat with Nora until his eyelids began to droop. She was curled on her side, breathing regularly, so he decided a cup of coffee was in order. Though he didn't want to leave her unattended, he reminded himself there was an officer at the door. She would be safe. Besides, he needed a shot of caffeine. Maybe it would supply an extra jolt of energy to keep his mouth in line. She needed help? She reminded him of thistles? *What's up with that, Seth?* Maybe it was seeing Nora thrown in the explosion. Maybe the trauma had jiggled loose something in his brain.

He'd fallen into the helper role before, with Tanya, only to be dumped for an edgier guy. Her boss. The same man whom he'd actually heard suggest to Tanya once after their breakup that she change to a more flattering outfit. Seth had spoken up, only to get a "stay out of it" glare from Tanya. She hadn't wanted his interference.

And neither did Nora, he reminded himself. Though it went against his grain, he had to remind himself not to overstep.

With a last glance to the sleeping Nora, he stepped out of her room and nodded to the cop at the door, then walked to the vending machine at the end of the hallway. Finding it out of order, he tracked down another in the opposite wing. Minutes later, when he finally returned to her room, he got the jolt he wanted. But it wasn't from the caffeine.

Both Nora and the cop were gone.

He set down the coffee with a thud, spilling half of it, and spun on his heel, sprinting back into the hallway. Now he caught sight of the cop at the nurse's desk exchanging information with another officer who had arrived to relieve him. But there was no sign of Nora. His eyes scanned the corridor. She wouldn't have snuck out, would she? Worse, had the bomber come back and taken her?

"Where…?" he started to ask, until in his peripheral he saw her getting into an elevator. He called to the cop, who realized his assignee was gone, and they both charged after her, but the doors closed before they reached them.

"I was only gone for two minutes," the cop explained.

Two minutes was plenty for an intelligent and resourceful woman to enact a plan.

"Where's she heading?" the cop demanded.

"Likely to her friend on the third floor. She probably figured out when you'd be switching with the other officer."

Seth beelined for the stairs. The cop jogged behind. After taking the steps two at a time, Seth emerged on the third floor in time to catch sight of Nora talking to the cop stationed outside Felicia's room.

When they caught up, she looked more defiant than chagrined, wrapped in a robe Kitty must have brought her.

"Before you start," she said, holding up a palm, "I got onto the elevator with plenty of other people. I did not lurk in empty hallways or use the ladies' room. Public areas the whole time and I stayed well within camera range." She pointed to the camera mounted above the third-floor nurses' station. "See? Safety precautions."

Seth drew in a calming breath. He should have known Nora was too smart to put herself in danger unnecessarily. But she had to realize someone still wanted her dead and whoever it was, was still at large.

The panting cop braced his hands on his gun belt. "You shouldn't have snuck out in the first place. You timed it to bolt during our shift change, didn't you?"

"Not bolting, just a quick visit. I have to see Felicia for myself."

"Her mother went home to change clothes," the cop at Felicia's door offered. "I think Ms. Tennison is asleep right now. She's been sedated."

"It will only take a minute," Nora insisted. "Please."

"No, you need to return to your room," her assigned officer insisted. "Right now."

Nora shook her head. No belligerence or disrespect, but plenty of determination. Seth could have told the officer that issuing orders wasn't going to garner any results with Nora.

Seth looked at both cops and shrugged. "She went to all the trouble. A minute with her friend won't hurt, right? With you two standing guard at the door?"

The doctor who was going about her rounds approved a quick visit. Both cops stood on the threshold and Nora and Seth went inside. He, too, was anxious about Felicia's condition.

Felicia lay on the bed, hooked to an IV and all the usual monitors. Her pulse was steady, blood oxygen good. One eye was swollen shut and one hand and arm was swathed in bandages. Half of her neck was bandaged as well, and the visible skin was red and crisscrossed with angry marks. Clumps of her hair had been burned away in the blast.

Nora gulped, clutching her robe around herself. Seth removed his jacket and draped it across her shoulders. She nodded her thanks but he could tell she was struggling not to cry as she leaned over the bed and touched Felicia's shoulder with a fingertip.

"Hey, Felicia," she squeaked then cleared her throat and tried again. "It's Nora. I had to see you for myself. I… I hope you're not hurting too much."

Felicia stirred and her eyelids flickered.

"She can likely hear you," he said. "But she may not be able to respond."

Nora stroked the burned clumps of Felicia's hair. "When we get out of here, you'll be able to get that short pixie cut you've been flirting with for years. It's gonna look chic on you." When there was no reply from Felicia, Nora looked around, her gaze landing on a bouquet of yellow carnations, their scent competing with the disinfectant. Seth followed her gaze and read the tag affixed to the stems.

"From Zane," he said.

"That's going to make your cheeks go pink when you wake up," Nora said to Felicia.

Felicia didn't answer.

Nora stroked Felicia's unbandaged arm. "I wish you could tell me what you'd found out. Then maybe whoever did this…" She swallowed hard.

Felicia stirred, her brow furrowing.

"Are you waking up?" Nora said eagerly.

Seth held his breath as Felicia's body began to move, her legs twitching. He'd seen dozens of different reactions as patients emerged from a medicated state. His sister Mara had told him that he'd been agitated, angry almost, when he'd first woken in the hospital after being shot.

"She might—" he started, but Felicia's eyes cracked open.

"Felicia," Nora said. "I'm here. I'm right here."

Felicia's lashes fluttered and she grabbed Nora's wrist, her nails digging into Nora's flesh.

"It's okay," Nora reassured her. "There was an explosion, but you're going to heal up just fine."

Felicia's eyes opened wider, one more than the other, and she looked wildly from Seth to Nora.

"Nora, this isn't a good idea," Seth said.

But Felicia was still clinging to Nora, her legs and arms now thrashing in agitation.

"No!" Felicia wailed. "No, no!"

"It's okay," Nora called, desperate.

But Felicia's low moans increased in pitch until Seth's ears throbbed. Her pulse rate began to climb on the digital readout.

He stepped toward the door. "Get a nurse," he told the cops, one of whom hastened off. Then he went to Nora's side and tried to ease her away, but Nora was imprisoned by Felicia's grasp, staring helplessly at her friend.

"Felicia," Nora cried. "What is it?"

"Where is he?" Felicia rasped.

"Who? It's just Seth and Nora here right now." Nora's face pinched with concern. "You're safe, honey. I promise."

"No!" Felicia screamed, the blankets bunching up around her. Her expression was wild, unfocused.

"Felicia," Seth said firmly. "No one is going to hurt you. Breathe in and out slowly, okay?"

A nurse rushed in and urged them all away from the bed.

Felicia's cries subsided into whimpers. She stopped thrashing.

"You both need to leave now please," the nurse said. "The doctor is on the way."

Seth took Nora's arm, noting the cuts where

magnanimous. I know what you are. If you touch my daughter again—"

Jude backed her farther away. "No more threats," he said, his voice like flint.

The doctor stepped out and spoke to Olivia, but Nora overheard.

"She's resting comfortably now," the doctor said. "But there are indications of internal bleeding. We're getting her into surgery right away."

Nora held back a whimper, but Seth must have sensed it since he tightened his hold. "It's okay," he said into her ear.

Bleeding. Surgery. The words blurred into a haze of fear.

Jude turned to Nora and spoke in a low tone. "Look. You can't be around Felicia, do you understand? I know you love her and this is hard for you, but no more. No one sees her but Olivia. Not you, or Zane, or anyone. Am I clear?"

His tone was firm and she could only nod. Her breathing was ragged, and she was still trying to hold back tears. Had her visit to Felicia sparked an outburst that worsened her condition? She couldn't stand to even think it.

As she tried to calm down, Seth told Jude what Felicia had said.

Jude frowned. "She said 'he came back'?"

"Yes," Seth said. "And I'll go ahead and say that it sounds like she's talking about Kai."

"Could be. But why would Kai care about Felicia and Nora? If his motive was to punish Zane for inheriting, or kill him to take the farm for himself, the women have nothing to do with that."

"Unless he's hoping to terrorize his brother into giving up the property."

Jude hesitated. "Or maybe Felicia saw Kai somehow and can testify to his criminal behavior. She's made someone scared or angry, that's clear. But I don't get why that would put Nora in the crosshairs."

Nora froze. He'd called her Nora, respected her decision to take her middle name. She should be pleased, but she felt cold and sick and small.

"We found a burner phone tossed in the shrubs near Olivia's place. Likely it was used to trigger the explosion. I doubt we'll get prints, but you never know. We also found this." Jude held up the bag. "I was bringing it to Olivia to see if she recognized it. Do you?" He raised the bag he carried so Nora could see what was inside it.

Nora shoved her hair back with a trembling hand and peered close. The cover was burned and one of the corners was missing, the pages badly warped. But she recognized it right away. "It's our high school yearbook."

"It was in Felicia's backpack that we recovered at the scene. Unfortunately, it's badly damaged. We'll go through it as best we can, page by page, and see if she made any notes or marks."

"Can I look too?" Nora said. "I want to help."

"Not right now. First the techs need to do their thing. It could be the lead we need." He shrugged. "Or it might have nothing to do with the explosion. Maybe she simply wanted to relive some good times. But Zane indicated he thought she wanted to meet to discuss Kai."

Nora chewed her lip. "I think she did suspect Kai. But there's no proof he's in the area, right?"

Jude didn't answer for a moment. "It's a big desert," he said finally.

The reply made the hairs on the back of Nora's neck prickle.

"Go on back to your room, Nora," Jude said. "I'll talk to Olivia and check in on you before I leave." He hesitated as if he wanted to say more. Instead he walked away.

Nora turned her head toward Felicia's room, but Seth eased her to the elevator with a guiding hand. She was still shivering and he snuggled her to his side, his body lending some warmth to hers.

"I…" she started then stopped.

"What is it?" he said as the elevator took them down.

Her first instinct was to clam up and retreat behind the safe bunker of silence. Instead, she gave words to the ache that filled her heart. "Like Olivia said, I've hurt Felicia. Maybe this *is* somehow my fault. I've damaged people in Furnace Falls, my family, Olivia…"

He turned her to face him.

"Nora, none of what happened to either of you since you hit town is your fault. There is a bad person out there—maybe Kai, maybe someone else—who almost killed both of you today. It's his fault, no one else's. Olivia is reacting out of pain and fear, looking for someone to blame. That's all. People need someone to target when their emotions get too big for them to handle."

She tipped her head and before she realized what he was doing, he suddenly pulled her close and kissed her cheek. Her heart beat a faster tempo, but just as quickly he released her and once again nestled her to his side. The sensation of his lips and the comfort of his embrace confused her. She wanted to surrender to the feelings he called up, but there was no place for emotions right now, she told herself, not for the first time. She simply had to get to her room and count the minutes until the day was over. Maybe she'd awaken and find out it was all some sort of a hideous dream.

A nightmare in which someone wanted her dead.

As the elevator descended, Seth berated himself for the kiss.

She needs you, but she doesn't want you. Two different things, remember?

Tanya had needed him, too, needed the stability of his presence through thick and thin, until she'd found someone she really wanted. This time, he told himself grimly, with this exceptional woman, he was not going to confuse *need* and *want*. Need made people stay close for a while. Want was the thing futures were built on.

Need, not want, and no more kisses, he told himself.

He and Nora didn't say anything further until they reached her room and she climbed back into her hospital bed with a wince. He knew her sore ribs were to blame.

"I'm sorry I snuck off to see Felicia," she said. "I won't do it again."

"Perfect, because that cop is onto your wily

ways now and so am I." He kept his tone light, reassuring, with a dab of friendliness, nothing more. He checked his phone, surprised to find it was almost six.

"Bubbles needs to be fed," Nora said.

Typical that she'd kept the animal's schedule in her mind in spite of nearly being killed. "I'll go take care of it."

"She might not cooperate with you entering her corral."

"I shall woo her with my cowboy charm."

Nora arched an eyebrow. "And if that doesn't work?"

"Then Levi will help me, but one way or the other, Miss Bubbles is gonna get her food and meds." He paused. "Then I'll come back." As soon as he said it, he knew he'd blown it again. What was he doing appointing himself her bodyguard?

She diverted her eyes, studying the bunch of thistles he'd given her. "No need. The cops are here. The doctors might discharge me tonight anyway."

He hid his doubtful look. "Sure, right. I'll check in with you later."

As he drove back to the ranch, he mulled over the last eight hours. The explosion, the violent confrontation with Olivia and Felicia's wild screams.

He came back.

He'll kill us both.

And the only thing standing between the bomber and Nora was a cop posted at her door. With a flash of determination, Seth decided that he was going to spend the night at the hospital, too, adding another set of eyes to the watchers. Nora didn't have to know of his decision and that eased his mind.

Just helping. No strings attached.

Bubbles was standing quietly in the encroaching dusk, ears pricked, when he rumbled onto the Rocking Horse. She watched him warily and he took things slow, like Nora had, while he replaced her bedding and refreshed her water and vitamin-laced feed. She'd need an injection in the morning and he'd have to get Doc or Levi to assist with that. Clearly, the donkey didn't trust him completely, but neither did she bolt to the other end of the corral.

Progress. At least he was better with donkeys than women.

Stopping in the kitchen for a sandwich, he found Levi drinking a glass of water. Banjo and Tiny snuggled on an old beanbag in the corner. Banjo thumped his tail at Seth but did not leave his warm spot. Bathed in lamplight, Levi appeared quiet and content, but he saw concern as Levi looked at him. "How are they?"

Seth filled him in.

"Is Nora coming back here when she's discharged?"

"If that's okay with you," Seth said.

"I'm not sure. That bomb came pretty close." Levi frowned. "Fine until Mara comes back. She's staying with Aunt Kitty overnight, but then, I gotta be extra careful."

"Extra careful?" Seth frowned. "Why…?" He suddenly remembered Mara's bouts of illness, the nausea, the fatigue she'd experienced off and on lately. His mouth fell open. "Are you two expecting?"

"Yes," he said with a smile.

Seth leapt from his chair and clasped his best friend in an awkward embrace that Levi deflected as quickly as possible. "All right then, simmer down," Levi said.

But Seth was exuberant. "I'm gonna be an uncle again. I can't wait."

"Well, you're gonna have to. Baby isn't due until June. Meanwhile…" He went to the closet and pulled out a rifle with the trigger guard in place and held it out to Seth.

"No," Seth said, "I'd rather not."

"This isn't about you anymore."

"Levi…"

His jaw set. "Seth, someone tried to kill Felicia and Nora. There's nothing to say they aren't planning to try again. If you're going to bring that situation onto this property, I'm counting on you to be prepared to protect the people who live here, my pregnant wife included." The blue of his eyes shone iron-gray in the weak light.

"If you don't want Nora to stay here, I'll arrange for another place," Seth said through the tightness in his throat.

Levi thrust the gun out further. "You're half owner of this ranch and she's Jude's sister. She stays, but you do your part."

His part.

Levi's tone softened. "It's time, man."

Seth knew Levi was right. Time to face it. He took the gun, cold in his grip, and the trauma flowed in again, the bullet shattering the windshield, plowing into his skull, narrowly missing his sister Mara. A bright flash of pain and then nothing except the terror of waking up unable to walk, to talk, even to feed himself. Levi brought him back.

"You're a crack shot, Seth. And you'll do what you need to do to protect the people you love. Even if you don't believe you can, I do."

The ferocious need to protect Nora infiltrated his every nerve. He had only recently met her face-to-face, yet he felt a deep connection that he could not explain. She'd already faced an ATV attack, a letter bomb, and now an explosion. Would he be able to defend her if it came down to another attempt? A cog clicked into place, settling into position something that had been out of alignment since the day he'd been shot. His muscles relaxed as he hefted the rifle. He would ensure her safety and his family's or die trying.

NINE

Every time Nora started to drift into sleep, alien hospital sounds yanked her awake. The cuts and scrapes throbbed with fresh pain as the minutes ticked on. Each tiny movement set off throbbing in her ribs. She was banged up and bruised for sure, but she'd sustained no injuries that wouldn't heal on their own.

Not so for Felicia who had been closer to the vehicle when it exploded. The memory of her being thrown back and hitting the ground before Nora lost consciousness would not relent. It killed Nora to know her friend was so damaged. Would she die? An urge bubbled inside her, the need to offer up her feelings to the Lord, but she pressed it down.

"He wouldn't help you even if you asked," she muttered to herself.

No matter what Seth might say, God was not here in the hospital room, nor had He been there when her world fell apart as a teen, or more recently, when she and Felicia almost lost their lives. The explosion had ripped free the scars from old wounds and inflicted new ones.

Fear circled like a silent panther, waiting to pounce when she fell asleep, so she didn't. Staring until her eyes burned, she fought the blanket of fatigue. Again and again she replayed the terrifying events. The ATV attack, the explosion.

Was Kai the culprit? And if so, why? She yanked the blanket up higher. If Kai was after her and Felicia, she intended to spot him coming. Thumbing her phone to life, she sought a photo of him online.

There wasn't much to go on. The only reference she unearthed was an out-of-focus image of him at a desert stock car race, one finger raised in the air to celebrate his victory. It was a black-and-white picture. He looked remarkably like Zane, body lean and angular, with a sweep of thick hair that he'd cut short in the front and longer in the back. Thinner than Zane, but probably as tall or taller. His lower jaw was swallowed up by an unkempt bushy beard.

What would Kai possibly want with Felicia and Nora? It was true that Felicia was rekindling a relationship with Zane. Might Kai be jealous? Had he been interested in Felicia from back in their high school days? Nursed an obsession ever since? But why would that put Nora in his crosshairs too? The car bomb might have caught Nora accidently, but the letter bomb had been certainly meant for her to find.

The yearbook might hold a clue, she thought. The one Felicia had been scouring would have a better photo, maybe some candid shots of Kai. Would Jude be able to salvage anything from the wrecked book?

The minutes ticked into restless hours. She thought of Bubbles. They had to be getting close to her delivery and Nora was seized with the need to be on the ranch, breathing in the crisp air and tending to the animal who had brought her to Furnace Falls against all good sense. Bubbles, she thought with a smile. Seth's nickname still amused her. She realized she again was picturing the lanky medic turned cowboy with the self-deprecating smile.

That's where she should be, the ranch. The thought made her flip the covers back until another froze her. Did she long to be on the ranch because Seth was there? No, not because of him, nor because of the fear that had taken root in her gut. Bubbles needed her and she couldn't stare at those hospital walls for one more minute.

It took her considerable energy to convince

the nurse and doctor that she needed to be discharged, but they finally relented. Pulling on her clothes, she considered the safest way to get to the Rocking Horse. A taxi? If there wasn't one outside the hospital, she'd call one and wait in the lobby. But first she'd text Jude her plans. That last bit grated since he would think her selfish and rebellious like he always had.

Her thoughts traveled back to one long ago day in particular, when she'd followed him up a precarious outcropping and been too scared to come down. He'd grabbed her hand and helped her, saying, *I'm your brother. I'm supposed to help you.* Now he likely wished her out of town for good.

She'd learned to live without her big brother's influence, so she might as well carry on regardless of his disapproval now too.

The second text would go to Seth and she hoped it did not awaken him since it was nearly midnight. Pulling on her clothes left her wobbly, the torn jeans and stench of smoke that permeated the denim causing her to gag.

Breathing slowly to steady herself, she texted Jude then Seth.

I'm coming back to the ranch now. Hoping this text doesn't wake you.

The three little dots and the immediate response surprised her.

I'll give you a ride.

No need. I'll get a taxi.

She pocketed her phone, opened the door and gasped. Seth stood on the other side, knuckles raised to knock, hair rumpled, T-shirt untucked, a sheepish grin in place.

"Talk about service, right?" Seth said.

Her eyes went wide. "You stayed here all night?"

He shrugged. "Nah. I went home and took care of that stubborn donkey, but I figured another set of eyes wouldn't hurt if someone was looking for trouble."

A hot flush crept up until it reached Nora's cheeks. Pleasure and anxiety warred inside her. "Oh," was all she could manage.

The officer at the door cleared his throat, getting her attention. "I'll follow you to the ranch," he said. "Jude's orders. He's...displeased."

An understatement, no doubt. They walked in awkward silence, which continued until they got into Seth's Bronco and drove through the wintry night. She was not sure what to say, how to feel. He'd assigned himself the role of her personal guard in spite of her wishes. Annoying and touching at the same time.

"I have a feeling I overstepped," he finally said when they were at the turnoff to the ranch.

"Yes," she said finally. "You did."

"I apologize."

She gave him a sidelong glance. "Why don't you sound sorry then?"

He frowned as if considering. "I am sorry if I made you feel uncomfortable, but I don't regret knowing that you're safe. I figured I'd sneak off before morning and you'd never know I was there."

She looked at him fully then, trying to summon up some righteous indignation, a suitable remark that would put him in his place for treating her like some helpless woman. Was he too self-absorbed to care? A chauvinist? Domineering? None of the labels seemed to fit Seth. The ire drained out of her. Was it the soft smile on his face, the shining earnestness that belied any sense of disrespect? She opened her mouth and then closed it. "You confuse me."

"I do?" His brows lifted in surprise. "How so?"

"I feel like I should be mad at you."

"But you're not?"

"No, for some reason I can't figure out." She sighed. "Must be tired, I guess."

He grinned. "Nah. It's cuz I got this natural magnetism. A cross between John Wayne and Gary Cooper."

She laughed. "That must be it."

He reached over and clasped her forearm, his smile vanishing. "I am sorry if I made you uncomfortable. I know I can be a bulldozer sometimes, when I think I know what's best for people I care about."

People he cared about?

The tires crunched onto the ranch property. Glimmering lights from the enormous tree added cheer to the velvety sky. In the moonlight, the mountains reached up to graze the stars.

"Beautiful, right?"

She nodded. "Yes, it is."

"Feels like coming home every time for me."

A pang of longing hit her.

He kept his hand on her arm, his touch light, and she didn't pull away this time. Confusing, she thought again. Seth, the ranch, and all the emotions he awakened in her. Just plain befuddling. She stepped out quickly when he parked, though it jarred her aching ribs.

Seth was unlocking the trailer door when her phone rang. "It's Jude," she said, tense. She pressed Speaker, figuring her brother would be more temperate with a third party listening. "You're on speakerphone with me and Seth."

"Bad idea to discharge yourself," Jude snapped without preamble. "I told you as much in the five texts I sent which you ignored."

"I read them, I just didn't reply." She heard him pull in a breath to continue his tirade. "What did you learn from the yearbook?" she said to divert him.

"Nothing so far. The pages are pretty much incinerated or gummed together. We'll locate another easily enough, but if Felicia left any messages or clues to what she was thinking in the book, they're gone." His tone mellowed the smallest degree. "Doc says Felicia is stable after surgery but she won't be able to talk to us for a while."

Nora exhaled. "That's great news." She swallowed. "Uh, thank you for telling me."

"You're welcome. I know she's important to you." It was odd, hearing her brother acknowledge her feelings, but the warmth soon dissipated. "Back to the point. I don't have enough cops to post one at the ranch, so…"

"You can deputize me," Seth said, turning the key in the trailer lock.

A couple of silent moments ticked away. "You want to take on protection duty?"

"Yes." Seth avoided looking at her as he pushed open the door. "I've got a rifle."

She was not sure what to say when Jude replied.

"I guess that will have to do for now. I'll let you know if we salvage anything from the yearbook."

"I have a yearbook too," Nora said with a start. "And an envelope of old candids stuck in the back, if I remember correctly. I'll look through it, see if I can find any photos of Kai. They're…" She gulped.

Jude quirked a brow. "At Mom's house?"

She felt her stomach tighten into a ball. "Yes."

She desperately hoped Jude would offer to retrieve them, but he didn't. He would not go the extra mile to alleviate the discomfort she'd undoubtedly earned, and he'd already made it clear she should avoid upsetting her mother. Well, there was simply no way Nora would be able to go ask her mother for the book personally. Her gaze wandered to the faint moonbeam that illuminated the cluster of trees not thirty feet from the trailer. The air went ice-cold and Jude's voice faded into the background.

"What is it?" Seth said.

"Nora?" her brother demanded.

She could not answer, transfixed by the silhouette next to a bent pine; a dark figure, the white gleam of a face, hat pulled low, shoulders hunched. There was someone watching them, watching her. Was that the hint of a beard?

Seth whipped around. "What is it?" he demanded again.

She blinked and the figure was gone. Stepped back into the foliage? A real intruder? Or merely her imagination?

"I thought there was someone watching from the trees."

Seth propelled her inside the trailer. "Lock the door and stay on the phone with Jude," he commanded.

"No, Seth. Don't—"

But he'd already grabbed the rifle and jogged away until she lost him in the night.

Seth had approached at an oblique angle, the weapon icy in his grip. He ignored the thundering of his pulse as he crept closer to the copse of trees. The cold air seemed to leech a chill into the rest of his body. Quiet as he tried to be, he could not avoid crackling the pine needles under his boots. Could he shoot if there was no choice, if it meant saving Nora or his family? Yes, he realized, though the thought of it sickened him, the weight of it, the responsibility. He detested holding a weapon in his hand that could also damage an innocent life, as it had his.

Goose bumps on his skin, he pressed on. *Lord*, he said with every step, *guide me*. One last cluster of slender trees remained between Seth and the only possible hiding place.

After a slow count of three, he darted around, rifle up and ready to fire.

There was only moonlight, the rattling of needles in the breeze. He checked under the shrubs, though they would have been too small to conceal anyone. Drifting through the trees, he examined every possible hiding place.

Whoever it was, if there had been anyone, was gone. Furthermore, he saw no sign of an intruder, no footprints, no broken branches. Were they hard to spot in the darkness? Or simply not there?

He returned to the trailer and Nora yanked the door open before he could knock. Phone in hand, she grabbed him in a tight hug. Heart thundering, he rested his cheek on her silken hair, stock-still in hopes of prolonging the moment. He had never felt such a sense of peace, of completeness, with any other person. The thunderclap of emotions stunned him.

When she moved back, she poked a finger into his chest. Her own cheeks were carnation pink. He hoped his feelings weren't plastered all over his face.

"You shouldn't have done that," she snapped. "You could have gotten hurt."

"There was no one there," he reported to her and Jude, who was still on the phone.

"Maybe I was mistaken."

"Who did you think it was?" Jude said.

She shook her head. "I was probably wrong."

"Answer the question," Jude demanded. "People have instincts for a reason. Who did you think you saw out there?"

Seth took her hand, cold as his own. "Trust yourself, Nora. Describe whoever it was."

She did. And then she pulled up the picture she'd found earlier on her phone and texted it to Jude before she showed it to Seth. A scruffy-faced Kai celebrating his stock car victory.

Bearded. And by all reports an angry young man.

Needles stabbed into Seth's stomach. If Kai was on the property… "Jude," he said, "if it's okay with Nora, I'm going to sleep on the couch in the trailer."

Nora opened her mouth to reply but Jude spoke immediately.

"Thanks, Seth. I'll send a unit over now, but that'd ease my mind."

Seth looked at Nora. "It's up to Nora. She gets the final word."

"Right," Jude said. "Whaddya say, sis?"

At the word "sis," Nora hunched a bit, wrapping her arms around herself. She no doubt wanted to decline his offer. Understandable; a private, determined woman fighting back fear as her world fell apart.

Her throat moved in a strangled swallow. "It's your trailer, Seth. I'm not going to tell you not to sleep in it."

Not exactly a ringing endorsement of the idea, but he'd take the win if it meant he could ensure her security. They hung up with Jude and Seth made sure all the windows in the back were locked. "I'll bunk on the sofa in the front room," he told her.

"I can take the sofa."

"Absolutely not," he said more emphatically than he'd intended. He tempered his next comment with humor. "Uncooperative patients who check themselves out of hospitals require comfy mattresses and privacy. Do you want anything to eat or drink?"

Nora shook her head. "A hot shower and a change of clothes will be perfect."

He activated the machine to fix himself a cup of the peppermint cocoa he'd stocked in honor of the Christmas season. It was more to keep himself busy than a desire for the beverage. His nerves were still skittering from his nighttime reconnaissance and her embrace.

She'd turned to go but stopped. Still not facing him, she spoke over her shoulder. "Jude... called me sis."

"Yes, he did."

"I never thought that would happen again. I felt like I'd lost him for good." The vulnerability struck him. For all her determination and hard-won independence, Nora still suffered from her teenage wounds.

"Could be God's making some room for reconciliation," he said quietly.

She went still then. Was she rejecting the idea? Had he sounded preachy? Or perhaps she was open to the possibility.

Lord, he thought, *let her feel Your strong presence in all of this*.

She turned a fraction more toward him, the lamplight catching the delicate curve of chin and cheek.

"I'm going to get my yearbook..." He heard her gulp. "From my mom's house. Tomorrow."

He waited. She didn't speak.

"Your mom loves you, Nora."

Her mouth pursed into a wobbly bow. "I hurt her. Badly."

"Parental love can withstand that kind of thing."

Now she jutted her chin toward him in a challenge, the brash Nora peeping through the insecurity. "How do you know that, Seth? You're not a parent, right?"

He chose his words with care. "I can't speak from direct experience, but I've noticed that when people become parents, they acquire this inner quality they didn't have before, a part that's tougher than diamonds, ferocious almost. I see it in my sister Corinne. I saw it in my own parents. It's this part that's made to love and believe and hope and endure, and forgive, no matter what." He tentatively reached for her, his fingers skimming hers, and drew her close enough that he caught the gleam of her tears. "It's a God thing. It's unbreakable."

"What if…?" she whispered. "What if you're wrong?"

He gently touched her under the chin and tipped her gaze to meet his. "I don't mean to sound arrogant, but I'm not wrong, Nora. Not about this."

The connection he felt in that moment was undeniable. Unable to resist, he allowed his lips to graze her forehead, purely a friendly gesture, yet it felt like so much more. "I'll take you tomorrow if you'd like me to." He hastened on. "Jude wouldn't want you to go anywhere alone."

She didn't answer, but for a fleeting moment he thought he noticed her relax. "All right," she said. "I'd appreciate it. You are an amazing man, Seth, and I'm glad I met you." Then she turned and left.

Amazing...glad I met you. The words thrilled him but there was a tinge of finality in them, as if a goodbye was hidden in the syllables. Well, of course it was. She'd been trumpeting her intention to leave ever since the day she'd arrived.

From the closet, he pulled out a pillow and a plaid blanket, though he did not imagine he would sleep much. He debated whether to wake Levi and tell him of the possible intruder, but since Jude was sending a police car to prowl the edges of the property, he figured it could wait until the morning. Banjo was on duty in the main house, so even if there was some kind of threat from Kai, no one would get the chance to cause trouble there.

He pulled the curtains back and stared out into the night. Quiet. Still. The corral was safely fastened and he could make out the silvered tips of Bubbles' ears visible in the little barn. Maybe Nora had been mistaken about what she'd seen.

But if she hadn't...the danger had come home to roost.

TEN

Nora slept, in spite of herself, waking at dawn to the sound of rain pattering on the trailer roof. *Mom...* The thought stabbed immediately into her consciousness, forcing her out of bed. Was there any possible way she could get out of it? Only by being a coward, she told herself. *You have to help Felicia, no matter how difficult it's going to be.* Face washed, hair secured and teeth brushed, she felt no more equipped to greet the day than she had before.

She forgot that Seth was on overnight guard duty until she almost tripped over him doing pushups in the living room. Stopping short, she waited for him to finish. His tall frame took up most of the space, the muscles of his back moving under the T-shirt.

He did a full set of thirty, gasping at the end, his right arm tremoring. When he collapsed on his stomach and then rolled over, he offered a surprised smile. "Oh. Morning. Didn't see you there." He sat up.

"Is that part of your therapy? Looks tough."

"No pain, no progress." He sighed. "I can get to thirty before the arm gives me trouble. At first I couldn't even do one, but I'm stubborn when I set about accomplishing something."

"We have that in common," Nora said.

"Yes, we do." Getting to his feet, he gestured to the tiny kitchenette. "Breakfast?"

"No thanks. I'm not hungry. I'll take care of Bubbles while you eat."

He washed his hands, grabbed a slice of bread and cheese and folded it together. Then he wrapped it in a napkin and shoved it in his jacket pocket. "I'll eat later."

She giggled. "You're gonna get crumbs in your pocket."

"Banjo will sniff them out. He takes his canine duties seriously." He grabbed the rifle and slung it over his shoulder and the figure she'd seen the previous evening lurking in the woods swam in front of her eyes.

The angst about visiting her mother had temporarily driven the other issue to the back burner but not for long. Someone wanted her dead. Fear trickled along her spine in a sickening rush as they left the trailer. Was that person out there now? The officer reported no sign of an intruder after his previous night's check. No tire tracks indicated anyone had driven onto the property. Then again, they could have snuck in on foot.

Or had it merely been her nerves twisting reality?

"Hey, Doc," Seth called.

At the sound of his voice, Nora shook herself away from the frightening thoughts. Doc was at the corral, his motorcycle parked nearby, his shoulders hunched against the rain.

"Morning." Doc's eyes were puffy, as if he had a cold or suffered through a long, sleepless night. "I was close, figured I'd check on the jenny. I want to give her another vitamin infusion."

"I'd offer you breakfast," Seth said as he withdrew the bread and cheese from his pocket, "but I think it might have picked up some lint from my pocket."

Doc waved Seth's offer away. Seth's eyes roamed the distance, the darkening clouds that promised more winter rain to come, but there was no sign of any strangers.

Banjo galloped up, skidding to a stop to bark.

"Awww, no need for that," Doc said, scrubbing Banjo's ears. "Remember I treated your burns after that porch fire. You and me are buddies now, right?" Doc offered him a treat, which he snapped up without even chewing, then set off to scour the tree line. Nora relaxed. If there was someone lurking, Banjo would sniff them out.

The vet tended the donkey while they looked on. Nora was pleased that Bubbles allowed the doctor to get close enough to administer the shot without darting away. The turnip he offered her won out over her distrust. Lips extended, she snagged it and backed into a corner to munch undisturbed.

"She'll be foaling soon," Doc said. "Good to see she's got an appetite, and the infection looks better. Maybe we're turning the corner here after all."

Nora relaxed a notch. Soon Bubbles would have her baby and be well enough to return to Colorado. But what about Felicia? How could Nora leave with her friend still in the hospital? With a potential killer still stalking them both?

Seth helped Doc close the corral gate. "Doc, you've been around town a long time. Did you know Kai Freeman, Zane's brother?"

"Not well," Doc said. He repacked his stethoscope into his motorcycle bag. "Rabble-rouser, I gather. Zane was supposedly the good guy of the two." Doc's lip curled.

Seth flicked a look at Nora. So he'd caught the odd response too?

"How well do you know Zane?" Seth asked. "You tend his animals, right?"

"He's doing that himself now, or maybe he's got an out-of-town doc. Doesn't need me anymore."

Perhaps Zane and Doc had parted ways and left some ill will behind? She thought of the motorcycle tracks she'd seen on Zane's property the night of the ATV attack. She noted the mud on the underside of Doc's motorcycle. But he was a country vet, so that went with the occupation. Likely she was dreaming up connections where there weren't any.

Doc continued. "Zane's got a fine setup. Date farm's lucrative. Everything's gone his way and not Kai's, so maybe there's some resentment there between the brothers." He turned to Nora. "Possibly you and Felicia got caught in the middle of that."

Seth frowned. "No, they were deliberate targets. What would either brother gain from hurting them?"

He shrugged. "Perhaps there's more to the situation than meets the eye. Zane was Mr. Dudley Do-Right in high school and he stuck up for his brother. Could be he isn't such a Do-Right anymore."

"What do you mean?" Nora said.

Doc shrugged. "People change. Animals don't. That's why I'm a vet, I guess."

"What people? Zane?" Seth edged forward a step, trying to get an answer, but Doc straddled his bike.

"Look," he said. "All I'm saying is Zane might have different motives than the young guy Nora and Felicia knew in high school."

Seth drilled into him with a hard look. "Doc, do you think *Zane* might have set off that explosion?"

He stared back. "I don't think he has the guts."

"But Kai does?" Nora said.

Doc shrugged. "Like I said, not my business."

"If it's Kai, he could be hiding out somewhere." Seth snapped his fingers. "Zane said his dog was missing. Kai might have taken it to terrorize Zane. Or maybe the dog went after him when he trespassed on Zane's property and Kai killed the dog."

Doc started the engine, not meeting Seth's eye. "Anything's possible," he said. "Bottom line is Zane and his brother are cut from the same cloth, so maybe they're both rotten. It's like they say in the dog breeding business...blood tells." He drove away without another word.

Blood tells.

The phrase roiled and bubbled in Nora's stomach as she and Seth got into the Bronco for the ride to her mother's house. Was Zane involved? Was Kai? And what was going on between Zane and Doc? A ton of questions, zero answers.

"The doc doesn't have any love lost for the Freeman brothers," Seth said as the truck sped along the smooth road toward Furnace Falls.

"No, he doesn't. Almost feels like they're enemies."

They lapsed into silence.

Nora got more tense with every mile they covered.

When they took the last turn off the main boulevard in Furnace Falls to a quiet road with a few houses, she drew in a slow, deep breath. Her childhood home hadn't changed much, except it was now painted a soft eggshell color with a burgundy trim. Maintaining a lawn was a losing battle in Death Valley. The front yard was the same rock garden that Nora had loved to prowl as a child. The twisted Joshua tree offered a small pool of shade, which in turn supported the growth of several scraggly shrubs. Amazing how life found a way to flourish even here.

Her hand quaked as she knocked on the front door. Seth applied a comforting palm to her lower back and gratitude filled her soul. She didn't deserve a friend like Seth. In fact, she'd visited problem after problem on him and still he was standing there in quiet support. Seth Castillo was a quality man, she thought. Attractive and sweet too.

Her stomach somersaulted as she heard shuffling from inside.

Kitty Duke opened the door, her generous mouth opening in surprise. A clip swept the fine hair away from her brow. She clutched at her baggy sweater with one unmatched button. Her mom would never think to buy a new sweater when she could mend the one she'd owned for decades. Nora wanted to stare at the button and will away the rampaging emotion, but she forced her gaze to her mother's face.

"Hi, Mom," she managed to say.

"Hello," she said. "This is a surprise." The words were tentative, as if she was trying to avoid spooking a wild animal that might dart away at any moment.

"I'm sorry to drop by."

A half smile etched the crow's feet deeper around Kitty's eyes. "You know I never mind anyone dropping by."

"Yes, I do." In her years of living there, Nora had never seen a single soul turned away. She'd witnessed her mother turn off a pan of frying chicken in mid sizzle in order to sit down and give her undivided attention to a surprise visitor. Then they'd finished cooking together and joined in the family meal. She was wired for hospitality.

I must have missed out on the genes for that, Nora thought. Her shared Colorado apartment had seen very few visitors except for friends Felicia brought over. Yet the Duke family had invited her right into their Christmas events, the tree lighting and dinner, and Seth had flung wide the door of his lovely trailer for her. They were hospitable people, in a welcoming town, so why were her legs shaking?

"Hello, Seth," Kitty said, finally pulling her gaze from Nora's face. "You're looking hearty and hale, sweetie."

Seth beamed. "Thank you, Aunt Kitty. God's been good to me."

She nodded. "We prayed so hard while you were in the hospital."

He took her hand and kissed it. "Much appreciated, as were all those meals and calls for my family. I believe all those prayers are why I'm standing here right now."

The peace and certainty that passed between them tickled something inside Nora. Imagine feeling so sure that God loved you. She'd maintained steadfastly for the past decade that God allowed her heart to break and so He wasn't on her side. Yet Seth's life had been tumultuous, and it seemed to only have cemented his faith.

And your mom had her life wrecked too.

Once by Dad, and the second time by Nora.

Just get in and out, she thought, struggling to hold her thoughts in check. *You're here to help Felicia. That's all.*

"Please come in," Kitty said, her fingers gripping the door for support as she backed up. Her legs seemed to be paining her, Nora surmised. How had her mother aged so quickly?

Not quickly, Nora realized. They'd been apart for a decade. The ten years had taken their toll. A strange mixture of sadness and longing washed over Nora at what she'd missed. *Get this over with.*

"I wondered if I could grab my yearbook," Nora said as they walked past Kitty into the house. The scent of fresh pine hung in the air. It wafted from the garland twined with red berries that her mother insisted decorate the mantel every year. The actual tree was artificial, since Kitty said it hurt her heart to cut down a tree that had managed to grow in the desert in spite of all odds, even though Jude insisted that the pines were trucked in from more temperate areas. Their mom was cheerfully stubborn about some topics.

Nora saw her own knitted stocking hanging next to Jude's. The sight of that raggedy red fabric made a stone lodge in her throat. Why would her mother still hang it after all these years?

"Will you have some coffee?" Kitty asked.

Seth darted a look at Nora, who declined. "Well, yes, ma'am," he said. "If it won't put you out."

"Happy to brew some up. It will only take a moment."

It occurred to Nora that Seth had realized her mother needed something to do, someone to serve, and he'd made that happen by asking for coffee. Seth was way more perceptive than Nora would ever be. She tried to breathe away the chaotic feelings that swamped her.

Kitty looked uncertainly to Nora. "I'm sure you can find your yearbook in a flash. Your room hasn't been changed."

Hasn't changed because her mother hadn't wanted it to. Why did that cleave Nora's heart? Unable to answer, she walked down the hallway.

Seth trailed her as she scurried to her tiny room where she was awed to find the twin bed neatly made, her "museum" still occupying a shelf. It was a collection of rocks squirreled away over her younger years, along with a pile of feathers. She fingered the journal where she'd sketched pictures from her pupfish adventures with Jude. Then there were the teenage touches: the headphones and flyers from the high school dances, a prom dress hanging in the closet. All frozen in time, a snapshot of happier moments when she'd been too naïve and selfish to appreciate what she'd had.

Oh, Lord… The prayer died away.

Kitty appeared in the doorway and handed Seth a mug of coffee. "I wasn't sure how you take it. There's cream and sugar."

"Just cream, thank you." He eyed Nora. "I'll pop into the kitchen and add a splash. Be right back."

Don't leave, Nora silently begged but Seth was already gone, and Nora was alone with her mother.

"Seth's a good man," Kitty said.

"Yes, he is."

She smoothed her palms on her sweater. "Did you find your yearbook?"

Nora couldn't answer.

"Here it is," Kitty said, pointing to a shelf with a couple of books. "I come in here and dust often," she said by way of explanation. "Why do you need it? Is it related to the attacks?"

"Honestly, I don't know, but I'm willing to

look anywhere to figure out who did this to me and Felicia."

She nodded. "Your brother is worried. And so am I."

Nora didn't know what to say to that. She grabbed the volume from her senior year, gesturing around the room. "I thought you'd have made it into a study by now or something."

"No," Kitty said. "I guess I was hoping you'd come home someday."

An ache settled under her ribs. "Mom..." She trailed off.

Her mother stared at her with an expression caught between hurt and pain. "Do you know what I've always wondered? Why the eighteen years didn't matter."

"What do you mean?"

Her fingers trailed over the painted white shelf. "I loved you and cared for you and we had a happy life until you found out about your father your freshman year. Even then I tried my best to be a good mother to you. When you finally left at eighteen, it was like you hated me, like none of those years of love mattered anymore."

Nora fought down the lump of guilt in her throat. "I was angry and hurt and I lashed out."

"I know that." She sighed. "And maybe I should have found a way to tell you before everything blew up, but I didn't want you to know what your father had done with…with the other women and your college money. I didn't want you to lose respect for him."

Nora looked at the floor. "It probably wouldn't have mattered if you'd told me because I wouldn't have wanted to hear it. I didn't believe Jude either. I couldn't."

"No, but then Jude isn't Mr. Sensitive."

They both chuckled.

Emotion swelled inside her, unlocked by their shared laughter. She felt the strong urge she could not identify; a push to loosen her grasp and let go of something painful so she could accept something better, kinder, gentler. She sucked in a shaky breath and turned to face her mother full-on. "Mom, all those years mattered. They still do."

A smile transformed her careworn face into the mother Nora remembered, the woman who had struggled with her own grief and betrayal. Tears glistened in her eyes. She reached out a trembling hand and Nora took it, her own fingers quivering.

"God's answered a prayer for me today," Kitty whispered, her voice breaking. "Just hearing you say that."

And Nora realized with a start that He'd answered one for her, too, one she hadn't had the courage to put into words. This was her mother, her precious mother, holding her hand. Kitty pulled Nora close and wrapped her in a tight embrace.

"I love you, Mom, and I'm sorry," Nora whispered into her mother's ear.

Kitty began to cry. Nora did too. With her mother's arms around her, it was as if the world wobbled on its axis and suddenly began spinning more smoothly, in the fluid motion for which it had been designed.

Seth popped his head in, mug in hand, took one look at their embrace and quietly withdrew. In that moment, she realized the reunion would never have taken place without him.

Thank you, Seth.

But not only Seth. She couldn't ignore the truth, that God had indeed made room for a reconciliation.

Thank You, Lord.

Seth drank two cups of coffee while he waited. He would have consumed a gallon if it meant Nora and her mother would have the time needed to work things out. He kept up a steady stream of sips and prayers until he was jittery from the caffeine.

Kitty arrived in the kitchen, nose red. "Well, she's found the yearbook."

Nora entered and took a seat. She didn't look at him, exactly, but he could tell she'd been changed by what had happened with her mother. He tried to keep his face from telegraphing his joy.

Nora laid the yearbook out on the kitchen table and was about to open it when a knock on the front door announced the arrival of Corinne and Willow with balls of yarn and knitting needles.

"Hi, Nora. We're here to knit Christmas stockings," Laney said. "Sure, it's last minute since Christmas is Friday, but better late than never. Aunt Kitty is going to advise, since Corinne is the only one of us who actually knows how to knit and she learned last week on YouTube. I'm providing moral support."

"Truthfully I'm here for the cookies Aunt Kitty promised," Corinne said with a smile. "Sugar cookies and ginger crinkles. I skipped breakfast."

Seth laughed and caught Nora's eye. "We were just leaving anyway."

Kitty walked them to the door and clutched Nora's wrist. "You come any time, okay?"

Nora nodded shyly and kissed her mom on the cheek, which unloosed a new flow of tears from both of them.

Kitty looked from Nora to Seth and back

to Nora. "This person out there, the one who blew up the car and tried to run you over. Until he's captured, you're not safe. Do you know what worries me the most, Nora? That I'll lose you again."

"You won't lose her, Aunt Kitty," Seth said. "I promise."

He guided Nora to the truck. He wanted to talk about what had happened, but Nora opened the yearbook as soon as she slid into the passenger seat. By the time they'd returned to the ranch, she'd thumbed through nearly all the pages.

"There's only one picture of Kai. He's working on a car in shop class. Then there's the one of Zane painting the sets that Felicia showed me earlier." She extracted a ragged manila envelope crammed in the back cover of the book and slid out a handful of Polaroids.

"This one's a silly shot of Felicia and Zane at a mini golf place. I don't see how any of these could hold a clue to what's happening now." She was still flipping through the Polaroids when they pulled up to the trailer on the ranch, drizzle streaking the windshield.

Levi rode a horse around the side of the corral to meet them, his face grave.

"Something's wrong," Seth said, cranking down the window.

"Donkey's gone," Levi said.

Nora gasped and shoved the photo under the sun visor. "How?"

"Dunno. Was the gate left open?"

She shook her head. "It was latched."

"Not anymore." Levi scowled. "No tracks that I can see. We'll go look for her. East or west?" he asked Seth.

Seth parked and leapt out. "I'll take the west, go as far as the wash. Nora, lock yourself in the trailer." Seth waited for her to get out.

"I'm coming with you."

"No, you're not."

"You need someone to watch your back and help manage the jenny if she's there. She doesn't trust you."

"I can do it, or I'll call Levi."

"It'll take him time to get to you."

"I—"

"I won't argue this, Seth. I'm coming. I'll phone Jude as we go." She strode ahead and he took her by the elbow. She whirled to face him. They were so close he could see the tiny specks of rain collecting on her lashes.

"This isn't safe," Seth said. "And…" And what? He'd been about to say that he would crumble if she was harmed. Dazed, he regrouped. "I promised your mom I'd see to your safety."

A raindrop trailed down her temple, but she didn't wipe it away, highlighting her glowing resolve. He expected a retort, or that she'd give him her back and hurry off. Instead, she took his cheeks between her palms and he almost stopped breathing.

"Seth, we're in this together. You're not taking risks in my place. You've been through enough." He was still absorbing the words when she placed a kiss, light as a down feather, on his lips.

Then she dashed into the trailer and a second later returned, zipping her jacket and running, hunched against the pelting rain. It wasn't until she'd grabbed a rope from the corral that he fought off the strange paralysis her kiss had caused. What had it meant? She was feeling the same attraction he was? Her words rolled through his memory. *You've been through enough.* She felt sorry for him, the damage from the shooting.

As quickly as the euphoria had grown in him, it ebbed away, leaving a hollow emptiness in its wake. *Well, what did you expect?* he told himself as he took up the rifle and ran after her. *You're merely a helper.* Need, *remember? Not want.*

Why did his dull brain refuse to learn that lesson?

ELEVEN

Nora still felt the tingle of Seth's lips on hers. Why had she kissed him? A moment of weakness? Gratitude? Worry? She gulped. Something deeper? Best not to mull over that one. Instead she focused on finding the donkey.

They ran together away from the corral and along a gradually sloping path that took them toward the distant wash. The raindrops coaxed silver from the flat ground and provided sheen for the dusky patches of green plants that took advantage of the moisture.

If someone had let Bubbles out of the corral, they likely had not been able to get a rope around her neck, so Nora figured she had to be wandering loose. In her condition... She swallowed a combination of fear and anger. Anything might befall a weakened jenny about to give birth. Had the intruder frightened Bubbles and got her to bolt from her corral?

Now it was rage that rose to the top as she

called Jude, explaining the scenario as quickly as she could. Seth was scanning the horizon, behind the Joshua trees, anywhere he thought someone might find a hiding spot. He was clearly worried about their exposure. So was Jude, who'd started in on a tirade.

"Absolutely not," he'd thundered. "Go back to the trailer immediately."

"Seth can't get the jenny by himself," she'd snapped before they'd ended the call.

Another person angry with her choice. But she couldn't let Seth risk his own life to save the jenny that had been her mission all along. He didn't deserve that. And Levi was also at risk as he rode his beloved ranch acreage looking for Bubbles. Jude was getting into his squad car even as she'd ended the call, so he'd arrive within fifteen minutes.

The trail emptied into a wide, shallow basin, a pattern of folded brown rock interspersed with prickly plants and a grove of trees. The vegetation here was deep-rooted, treated to bouts of occasional flash flooding alternating with the ferocious dry season. The sweep of twisted ground folded together like an elaborate plaited bread dough and some hundred feet away was a cluster of creosote bushes grown to well over ten feet tall. Nora found what she was looking for; a hoof print in a mucky portion of ground heading in the direction of the thicket. "She'd have gone there for shelter from the rain."

Seth drew her into the shadow of a pile of rocks. "Agreed. Give me the rope and I'll get her."

"She won't—"

"Cooperate? Probably not. I don't have your way with burros." He scanned the area yet again. "Let me go first and check it out. If she won't go along with the plan, I'll call for you." He crept away.

Nora didn't like the idea of him going alone, but she could tell by the set to his jaw she wasn't going to dissuade him. Whoever had freed Bubbles might be hiding in the foliage, planning some sort of ambush.

Would Seth sense an attack coming at him from the shadows? Intently staring in his direction, she was jerked from her reverie by the sound of a boot scraping against the rock. Had he doubled back? Or maybe it was Jude?

The thoughts died away as a man appeared around the edge of her sheltering rock. He wore a ski mask, but a hint of beard protruded from the mouth hole. He stared, hands fisted at his sides.

Cold terror swamped her. She didn't see a

weapon. Running would be her best option. She edged out a step from her rock shelter.

"You don't belong here in Furnace Falls," he said, his voice low, menacing.

Icy terror prickled her flesh. The man was the one hiding in the trees the previous night. She'd been right; he had been watching, listening even. Nora moved a fraction more. "Why are you after me and Felicia? What did we ever do to you?"

He didn't answer, shaking his head slowly from side to side. Nora moved her phone slightly and tried to slyly press 9-1-1, but he shot out a hand and struck her on the wrist. The phone clattered to the rock.

As she started to run, he grabbed the back of her jacket.

She only had a moment to react. She stopped abruptly and brought both her elbows slamming backward where she hoped his face would be. She'd misjudged. The blow caught him in the chest and she heard the breath whoosh out of him, but it was enough to cause him to loosen his grip.

She didn't wait for him to regroup, sprinting away in the direction of the thicket.

She heard him lunge for her but dared not look back. "Seth!" she screamed. Stumbling, she went down on one knee as Seth emerged from the bushes. He ran toward her, eyes wild, rifle ready.

"What?"

She stabbed a finger toward the rocks.

"He almost caught me."

Seth didn't stop to ask who. He ran to the rocks, disappearing for a few moments. She got to her feet, brushed off her clothes, arms stinging from the defensive move. She'd struggled to catch her breath by the time Seth returned, pain flaring in her bruised ribs.

"Only saw his back before he got away," he said.

He guided her to the rock shelter and called Jude. He told the chief about the attacker.

"Just turned onto the property," Jude said. "I'll get him."

Then Seth called Levi and filled him in. "Bubbles is here too," Seth added before they disconnected.

Nora sighed in relief. "At least we found her. She okay?"

He nodded. "She's in the trees." He helped her locate her phone before he led her to an area under the dripping boughs. Bubbles was crammed close to a tree, trying to avoid the drizzle. Water ran down her neck, and she appeared miserable.

Nora readied the rope, her fingers still shaking from the violent encounter. "Okay, little mama. I'll get you back home where it's warm and dry, but you're gonna have to trust me."

Bubbles shifted backward until her hind end brushed the trunk. Seth was the lookout, his gaze roving the area for any sign of her attacker.

"Gotta make this as quick as we can, Nora," he murmured.

"Here, honey," she said as the donkey's ears started to flatten. If she bolted past Nora, there wasn't much either of them would be able to do to get her back to her corral.

Time for the big guns. Nora reached into her pocket for a peppermint and unwrapped it. Candy wasn't the healthiest treat for equines, but it was all about the greater good at the moment and Bubbles had proved she had a sweet tooth. The donkey's nostrils quivered at the scent of the confection and her tongue whipped out and snagged the sweet. Munching contentedly, she allowed Nora to slip the rope over her neck and nudge her away from the shelter. Every few feet, Bubbles would plant her hooves and dig in until Nora offered another peppermint.

It was a slow process that caused Seth enormous stress until Levi galloped up with his rifle over his shoulder.

Seth's shoulders relaxed an inch. "Glad to see you, Levi."

Levi nodded. "Let's get her home."

Levi scouted while Nora coaxed Bubbles onward with Seth encouraging from the rear. She'd used up her last peppermint by the time they made it back to the corral. With enormous relief, she guided Bubbles through the fence into the barn. Levi entered as she'd finished filling the trough with grain.

"I'll tend to her," Levi said. Without waiting for her reply, he approached in that quiet way of his and gingerly patted Bubbles dry as much as she would accept. Though Nora was still shaking inside, she was pleased that Bubbles would now tolerate some level of human handling. Then again, Levi had an uncanny gift that meant animals of every kind trusted him.

"Thank you," she said.

He nodded, not taking his eyes off Bubbles as she returned to the trailer. Jude arrived and he and Seth ushered her inside where she peeled off her sodden jacket. The warmth was blissful and she sank down on the kitchen chair Seth slid out for her. They followed suit.

"No sign of him," Jude said, his tone clipped. "Who was it?"

"I'm pretty sure it was Kai," Nora said. "Facial hair, same height and build." A thought occurred to her. "But it isn't that hard to put on a fake beard. Could it have been someone else? Zane and Kai look alike." But there was still no motive that made sense to her for Zane to act in such a way.

"I'll go talk to Zane right now," Jude told her. But she could tell her brother did not put much stock in the idea that Zane was involved.

"Doc doesn't have fond feelings for either brother," Seth said.

Nora stared in thought at the tabletop. "Felicia said 'He came back,' so that makes me think it's Kai." She paused. "Could Doc have something to do with it, though? We saw motorcycle tracks on Zane's property the night we were almost run down by the ATV."

"Doc?" Jude grimaced. "Way too farfetched."

"The whole thing is farfetched," Nora snapped. "But I'm not going to reject any theory."

"Leave the theory building to me." Jude tapped the tabletop. "It's my job."

"It's my *life*," Nora retorted. She saw anger kindle in his expression, the thick-necked, bull-headed stance he got when he believed he was right.

He folded his arms across his broad chest and she saw the bunching in his jaw muscles. "Excuse me if I'm struggling to keep up with all this. You've been gone for a decade and now you're in town, under attack, and I'm sorry if that makes me edgy."

She blazed a look at him. "Because your little sister is causing trouble?"

"No," he snapped. "Because I'm afraid my little sister will get hurt."

She blinked, watching the flush in his cheeks, which no doubt mirrored her own. He was afraid she'd get hurt? Where there had been anger and resentment, there was suddenly something else. She wasn't sure what to say.

He shot an exasperated look at the ceiling. "I forgot how stubborn you are."

A laugh escaped her. "I was thinking the same thing about you."

His lips curved in a fleeting smile. A temporary truce. "What did you find at Mom's? There must have been a clue in there."

"Not that I can tell, but maybe in the extra photos." She frowned. "How did you know I found something?"

"Two reasons. Mom called me, said you were there." He jerked a thumb out the window toward where Seth had parked. "And there's the other problem I haven't had a chance to tell you about." He led them outside to the Bronco.

Bits of glass glimmered in the wet dirt like fallen stars. The side window of the Bronco had been bashed in with a rock that now lay on the passenger seat. The yearbook and the accompanying manila envelope of photos were gone. Nora resisted the urge to shout in frustration. They'd been led a merry chase, following Bubbles, while someone—Kai?—had slipped back to the truck and stolen the photos. Or had an accomplice do it.

She recalled the man she'd seen in the trees. "He was listening when we discussed it on the trailer porch last night. He knew I was going to Mom's to get the photos and he set up the theft." She felt like shrieking. What if one of those images might have held the key? Now they had nothing to go on. A few seconds later, she remembered. Reaching in, she flipped down the sun visor. "At least he didn't get this one." She held up the photo of Felicia and Zane.

Seth and Jude crowded close and Jude took a picture of the photo before giving it back to Nora. A siren echoed up the trail.

Levi returned from drying Bubbles and observed the broken glass. "Springing the donkey was a diversion?"

"Looks that way," Jude said.

"Bubbles okay?" Nora asked.

"She let me rub her down pretty thoroughly before she told me to get lost. She's warm and dry. Wouldn't hurt for Doc to check her out when he can."

Jude waved them off as his phone rang. "I have to take this. Nora, I know you're all tough and independent, but would you mind staying in the trailer until I get more people here?"

He'd asked instead of ordered, which took some of the starch out of her spine. That and the memory of his earlier statement. *I'm afraid my little sister will get hurt.*

"Okay."

"I'll find a padlock for the corral," Seth said. "Don't worry."

How had he known that was what she was thinking about? She did not want Levi or Jude to see the vulnerability on her face. Chin ducked, she walked behind Seth, who held the trailer door open for her.

"Sis," Jude called, palm over his phone before she stepped inside.

She spun. *Sis?*

"That was a brave thing you did, talking with Mom. It made her happy." He paused and she saw him swallow. "And it made me happy too. I, um, I know I didn't handle things right back then. You were a kid and I forgot that." He sighed. "Anyway, I'm sorry."

"Me too," she murmured, her heart suddenly full.

Seth squeezed her shoulder before he went to fetch a padlock. The gentle pressure spoke volumes. He understood what Jude's words meant. He was the kind of man who would.

She closed the door. For a moment, she leaned her forehead against the metal, awash in a barrage of feelings.

Fear, the memory of Kai's hands gripping her jacket.

Triumph, that Bubbles had allowed herself to be led to safety.

Hope, to think there might be a mending in her family.

Pleasure, from her kiss on Seth's lips.

The happy feelings were overshadowed as another took their place. Uncertainty, about her fate and Felicia's, the missing photos, the threats that seemed to have no motive. How could this time in Furnace Falls bring out such terrible and wonderful emotions simultaneously? She clutched the picture, the only one that had escaped the intruder. Holding it under the kitchen lamp, she studied every inch of it.

The photo caught a smiling Zane, who'd just tossed a golf ball up into the air, right palm open and ready to catch it, mouth pinched in a comical expression. Felicia looked on, holding her own club like a baton ready to be twirled. There was a shoulder in the picture, a yellow

T-shirt and the curl of reddish hair visible. Kai? Perhaps. And who had taken the picture? A random stranger? When Felicia had started dating Zane, Nora had been busy with her own life, working at the local stables, dating a few boys now and again. She hadn't gone on the mini golf excursions, but Felicia was an avid photographer and made sure to give Nora copies of every picture.

She stared at the photo until her eyes burned. Late that night, with Seth installed on the couch, she examined the photo again for the millionth time. But if there was any clue, any at all, she could not find it.

The next day passed in slow motion with the cops coming and going and ranch chores begging to be done. Levi called in a favor and the window of Seth's vehicle was quickly repaired.

It galled him that he'd been tricked so easily, but how could he allow a heavily pregnant and ailing Bubbles to wander the property? Why had the stalker needed the photos anyway? Seemed like a risky waste of time. Another yearbook could be located, no doubt, but maybe there had been something in the loose photos that might have proved incriminating. Was it a local then? Zane? Kai? Olivia hated Nora too. Instinct niggled at him. What about

Doc? He'd certainly been acting odd, but Seth could not think why he would have any reason to harm Felicia or Nora.

At night he and Nora shared a simple meal of chili and biscuits that he'd brought back from the main kitchen. "Levi said to get it out of the house before Mara comes home since she suddenly can't stand the smell of garlic," he said, chuckling.

Nora's mouth rounded into an *O* as she read between the lines. "Wait. Are you going to be an uncle again?"

"Yes," he said proudly. "Uncle Seth's gonna have a new protégé."

She smiled. "That's fabulous news. Congratulations."

He was pleased to see her genuine pleasure. It lifted the gloom for a few moments anyway. Though he couldn't quite forget her kiss from yesterday, she gave no indication that it had meant anything more to her than a friendly gesture, so he tried to shoehorn it from his mind.

She lapsed into quiet as they cleaned up from the meal.

After dinner, she disappeared into the bedroom. He watched the day mellow into night and the stars shimmer to life. The distance from most metropolitan light pollution laid bare the constellations as if a curtain had been pulled back. He wished Nora was beside him to enjoy the luminous Milky Way.

When she emerged from the bedroom an hour later, he was lying on the couch, attempting to read a book, glasses perched on the end of his nose. He whipped them off quickly, in case it made him look like a wizened old man, which in turn made him rue his own vanity.

"What are you reading?" she asked.

"Donkey care for dummies," he said, sitting up. "You okay?"

"Couldn't sleep. I was poking around online. Did you know there are sites where you can search old yearbooks?"

"The power of technology. Find anything interesting?"

"I keep going back to this one." She sat next to him on the couch and showed him her phone. The feel of her warm side brushing his shoulder made his pulse quicken.

The photo was a candid shot of Zane painting what looked to be the backdrop for a play, some Venetian city maybe. Splotches of blue paint showed on the brush in his right hand, a dripping paint can in his other. Photobombing the picture was his brother Kai, two fingers up in a peace symbol. Seth squinted at Kai, unwilling to put on his reading glasses in front of her. Kai had a scruff of facial hair, and his frame was stockier than his brother's.

"Can you tell if he was the one who attacked you at the wash?"

Nora sighed. "I think so but I can't be positive."

Seth pointed to the image below, a page from the show's program. He read the names listed there. "Looks like Felicia had a minor part. Zane was crewing the show."

Nora nodded. "That's how they met, in the drama club."

"His brother isn't listed on the program." One name surprised him. "Olivia worked on the show too?"

Nora frowned. "I didn't know that. I wasn't the acting type and I was caught up in my family drama."

Seth enlarged the tiny writing with a flick of his fingers. "Says here she helped sew the costumes."

"Likely. She was involved in Felicia's life as much as Felicia would allow it. Felicia was adopted as a baby and her dad died when she was a toddler. Her uncle stepped in to help, but Olivia was her main caregiver. Why? What are you thinking?"

"Nothing really," Seth said. "Just noticing that Olivia had a connection to Zane and Kai."

Nora frowned. "She can't have anything to do with this. Olivia would never harm Felicia."

"Maybe her target was someone else."

Nora turned to him. "Me? Why would she? Aside from her obvious hatred of me, that is. But a car bomb is pretty extreme."

He waved a hand. "I'm not a detective. Just shooting off my mouth, is all. I wouldn't think she'd do anything that might harm Felicia either."

But could she have asked Kai to kill Nora? Because she knew Felicia was likely to leave town again after the holidays unless things got serious with Zane? Maybe Kai had messed up, rigged the wrong car to explode. He wondered if he was letting paranoia take hold.

When they couldn't stare at online yearbook photos any longer, Nora put the phone down. "I'll tell Jude what we talked about as soon as I can. He'll listen, I'm pretty sure." A tiny smile curved her lips and he knew what she was thinking about.

"Things are going well with your mother and brother, aren't they?" he said softly.

Tears deepened her eyes to the shade of lapis lazuli. He wanted to capture a memory of that hue so he could picture it forever.

"We have a long way to go, but I feel hopeful for the first time since I left home." She took his hand and squeezed it. "Thank you, Seth. You helped me get my family back."

He savored the delicate strength of her touch. "God did that."

"I…" She swallowed. "Yes, He did, with a nudge or two from you. I'm ready to accept that now."

Happiness ballooned in his chest. "I'm thrilled for you. Completely."

"I know you are." Again the lapis drew him in.

His heart leapt. Her life had changed, and maybe her mind had too? Maybe the kiss had meant more than he'd thought.

He wanted to loop his arm around her, to bring her closer and feel her soft hair, and kiss her properly. The connection between them couldn't only be obvious to him, could it? He was leaning closer when Nora's phone rang.

She answered it on the first ring. Her brows puckered as she listened. "Um, sure. Yes, of course. I'll be right there." She disconnected. "It was Olivia. She wants me to meet her at the hospital."

Now his brows were puckering too. "Why?"

"She didn't say."

"When?"

"Right now."

Why would a woman who had physically

threatened Nora and blamed her for her daughter's misfortune want to chat?

"I'm not sure…" he started, but Nora was already on her feet.

"I'm going to do anything I can for Felicia, and if that means talking to her mother, I'll do it." She grabbed her jacket.

He felt that thrill again as he watched her stride to the door, her expression brimming over with the love of her friend and the determination to help. He loved that about her.

Loved?

How had that word popped into his head? Why not fondness, affection, a growing sense of appreciation?

Nope, none of them felt like a proper fit. And that wouldn't do. Not at all.

He yanked his jacket zipper up so fast it pinched his chin.

Good. Maybe the pain would snap him back to good sense. And put his mind back where it needed to be.

He led her out of the trailer, his hand up to forestall her argument. He was going with her. He wouldn't let her out of his sight, not with a killer on the loose.

TWELVE

Nora tried to quell the trembling in her body as they made their way to the hospital waiting area down the hall from Felicia's room. Nora wished with everything in her that she could stop and see her friend, but Olivia had forbidden it. So why the meeting now? Seth walked with his arm linked through hers, which she suspected was the only reason her legs hadn't given out. She clung to him more tightly than she should have.

In a quiet corner they found Olivia. She was clearly exhausted, but her hair was neatly braided and she wore fresh clothes. She didn't get up from her chair, instead gesturing Nora and Seth to take seats opposite her. "You don't need to look at me like I'm a wild animal. I'm in control now and I'm not going to attack you."

"Yes, ma'am," Seth said and there was a steely quality to it, as if he was saying, "You got that right." She felt a flush of pleasure at his protectiveness. There was no apology from Olivia for her earlier threats but Nora hadn't expected one. She didn't blame the woman, not after what she'd witnessed after the car exploded.

"Felicia woke up once only for a few seconds. And she asked for you," Olivia said, articulating precisely, as though the sentence cut her mouth as it exited.

Nora fought her constricting lungs for a breath. "How is she?"

"Scared." Olivia crossed one leg over the other. "That's why I asked you to meet me. Just to be clear, I don't like you any more than I did before. I know in my bones if it weren't for you, my daughter would be with a dance company somewhere like she'd dreamed of, and she wouldn't be lying in a hospital bed."

Nora swallowed hard, but she forced herself not to look away. Some of the situation she owned and some she didn't.

Seth held up a palm. "Mrs. Tennison, this isn't productive when there's a potential murderer out there planting car bombs. That's who we should be focused on. Did you know there was an intruder on the ranch who tried to attack Nora last night?"

Olivia sat up straighter. "Who?"

"I think it was Kai," Nora said.

Olivia remained silent for a moment. "I asked you to meet me here because Felicia's scared, like I said, and I realized that the threat to her isn't over."

"Not to Nora either," Seth said.

"Agreed. I promised when I adopted Felicia as an infant that I would protect her with my last breath. Someone needs to pay for what they did. The police told me the bomb was placed in a way that would have killed you both." She shifted. "I need to find out who did it and you're the only one who might have a clue since Felicia can't tell me right now. I want to know who tried to kill my baby. Do you believe it was Kai?"

"I think he was the person who attacked me last night. It was raining and somewhat dark, and he wore a mask when he came after me." She stared at Olivia. "You knew Kai," she countered. "In the yearbook there were photos of the drama productions, and you helped with the costumes. What did you think of him?"

Olivia tapped a finger on the arm of the chair. "Impulsive. A low achiever, the kind of person I didn't want around my daughter."

Nora ignored the harsh answer. "Did Felicia spend time with him?"

"Not really. She wasn't interested. I was glad

when he got sent away. His mother made the right choice. I would have done the same. But what reason would Kai have for hurting Felicia and you? He hasn't been in town for years."

"Not sure. I didn't even know him in high school."

"Maybe Kai is jealous of Zane and wants to punish him," Seth suggested. "Zane inherited the farm instead of his brother."

"What does Zane say about Kai?" Olivia said.

"Defends him mostly." Seth seemed to consider his answer for a moment. "Appears as if he's struggling to accept that his brother might be involved."

"Well, he's gonna have to, isn't he?" Olivia snapped.

"Hello, all," a voice said, startling Nora.

Zane stood there in khakis and a worn tee, holding a bunch of pink roses. "I was trying to visit Felicia. But I still can't get by the cops," he said. His gaze shifted between the three of them. "Am I interrupting something?"

Olivia eyed him. "We were just talking about you, actually."

His eyes rounded, gleaming in the overhead lights. "That right?"

"Yes." Olivia folded her arms. "I'm wondering if what happened to Felicia has something to do with you or your brother."

His brows creased. "You don't beat around the bush, do you?"

Olivia didn't seem to hear. "Felicia was only back in town for a short while before the incidents, but she'd been messaging and calling back and forth with you, right? Did you tell your brother about it?"

"No," he said. "I haven't spoken to my brother since he left town, as I've told everyone who's asked. His choice. I tried to contact him many times but he never responded. When Felicia reached out, it caught me by surprise, honestly. We had fun in high school, but things didn't pan out. When she ran away from town, I figured we weren't meant to be."

"I agree," Olivia said. "I'll admit I discouraged Felicia from seeing you back in high school."

Zane's mouth fell open. "Why?"

Olivia sighed. "She wanted to dance and there was no future for her here in Furnace Falls. This is an isolated town with zero opportunities for a dancer."

Zane stared at her. "So what you're saying is I would have slowed Felicia down?"

"Not to be rude, but yes."

Zane arched his brow. "That *is* rude and

judgmental. Small-town kid not good enough for your daughter?"

"Small-town kid with a bad-news brother," Olivia corrected.

Nora saw Zane flinch.

"Kai never had a chance, did he? Mom sent him away because she knew no one would give him a fair shake here."

"I don't have the time or energy to sugarcoat things, Zane," Olivia said. "Let's just speak plainly. Your mom sent Kai away because he was expelled from high school and she couldn't control him. He was a lost cause."

The color rushed to Zane's cheeks. "Don't talk about my brother that way."

"I'll talk about him any way I want, and if he's involved in hurting my daughter and you're protecting him, you better hope I never find out." Her eyes burned.

Bitterness seeped into Zane's tone. "And you wonder why Felicia stayed away for a decade. She never should have come back here."

Olivia's lips thinned into a tight line. "She wanted to reunite with you, Zane. The donkey was just an excuse." She stared directly at him. "I'll ask again. Did your brother hurt my daughter?"

"Kai wouldn't do that," Zane insisted.

Nora watched for any tells on Zane's face,

but all she could detect was frustration. She'd feel the same if someone accused her brother and she felt helpless to defend him.

"Was Kai jealous then?" she demanded. "Maybe he wanted Felicia, but she was smitten with you so he got mad."

"I would never let anyone hurt Felicia. I loved her since the ninth grade. She came back. I thought I was getting a second chance and if Kai was around he'd be happy for me." He cocked his chin. "But obviously you wouldn't want that."

"Correct." Her tone was cold and flat. "Nothing personal."

Nora and Seth exchanged a look.

Zane's eyes narrowed and his lips thinned as his gaze sharpened on Olivia. "You say Felicia's too good for Furnace Falls and for me and you'd do anything to keep us apart. So just how far would you go, Olivia? Is there anything *you* need to confess?"

"What are you getting at?" Seth said.

Zane continued to glare at Olivia as he answered. "She sits there spouting accusations about not wanting Felicia and me to get together. Could be she arranged the ATV attack and the bomb thing to scare Nora off and it went wrong."

Olivia rose to her feet. "How dare you imply I'd hurt my own daughter!"

"Nothing personal," he mimicked with venom. He glanced at the flowers in his hand and dropped them on a chair but they fell onto the floor. Nobody moved to pick them up. "I don't suppose you'll give these to Felicia, but at least tell her I came to see her…if that's okay for a small-town boy to do." He spun on his heel and he'd made it only a few paces when a doctor strode up, his face grim.

"May I speak to Mrs. Tennison privately?" he asked.

Heart thudding, Nora followed Zane and Seth a few paces away. Nora hugged herself, terrified. Whatever the doctor had come to say wasn't good news.

Beside her, she heard Zane gulp and she followed his gaze, seeing a bustle of activity—two nurses and a doctor headed into Felicia's room.

"I'm getting a bad feeling," Zane said. Nora found herself patting his shoulder. Olivia had been brutal and Felicia would've been mortified at her mother's treatment of the man she had feelings for.

Seth took her hand and they stood there, linked together, the moments edging along in slow motion. Nora saw the doctor bend toward Olivia, his tones soothing, low.

Then Olivia recoiled, her expression stark even from a distance.

Nora realized she was holding Seth's fingers in a death grip. "Just keep breathing," he said, his tone impossibly reassuring.

The doctor finished with Olivia and nodded at them as he passed and vanished into Felicia's room. Olivia walked over to them. Her eyes burned like coals against her pallid complexion. "Felicia's got an infection now," she said. "They've put her in a medically induced coma."

Coma? The word was so hopeless, terrifying. "What…?" Nora's question trailed away.

"They're going to airlift her to a Las Vegas hospital," Olivia said. "But…"

Zane's voice came out like a croak. "But what?"

Olivia's voice was flat, almost robotic. "The doctors are not optimistic."

Zane grimaced. "Not optimistic? What does that mean? They don't think she's going to make it?"

Olivia's gaze traveled slowly to Zane. "She's going to make it. She has to." The desperation was palpable and Nora reached out reflexively, but Olivia strode away.

"Is Felicia going to die?" Nora whispered. Seth tucked her to his chest and spoke softly against her hair. "God knows and He loves her more than we do."

Wracking sobs bottled up in Nora's throat. She held them in but tears began to roll in hot trails down her cheeks. "I... I want to pray," she breathed.

"Come on," Seth said, turning her in the circle of his arms and propelling her forward. "I know where the chapel is."

Nora looked at Zane, who stood staring at the door to Felicia's room. His hands were shoved into his pockets, his face like stone. The pink roses still lay on the floor, bright against the dingy background. She felt a surge of pity.

"Why don't you come with us?" Nora said.

Zane shook his head. "No, thanks. I'll wait here. Olivia can't toss me out. Public building, even for small-town nobodies."

Nora couldn't stop the tears as Seth led her into a tiny chapel. In the corner there was a small table with a battery-powered lantern and a simple swag of pine and holly. She sank into a chair. "I can't think..." she whispered, unable even to manage the simplest of prayers. She turned her tearstained face to his. "Will you?"

Seth sat next to her and took her hands. He began to pray. Silently, fervently, sincerely, Nora joined in.

They stayed in the chapel until Felicia was transported. Nora had been so unsteady witnessing her friend strapped in a stretcher with all the tubes and monitors attached, she needed Seth's supportive arm to make it back to the Bronco and to the ranch.

He'd been miserably uncertain about how to comfort her. Tea? Warm blankets? More prayer? Should he get Mara in case she'd feel more comfortable talking to a woman? Or maybe Jude or Aunt Kitty? He plugged in the silver tree in the corner of the trailer and the colored bulbs cast a warm glow.

She smiled when she saw it. He was happy he'd helped a tiny bit. "This really is a beautiful place," she said, her glance taking in the view of the massive Christmas pine through the window.

More beautiful with you here, he thought. "The desert is spectacular in December."

She nodded, specks of tree light reflecting in her eyes. "In spite of everything, I believe you're right."

His heart beat with something like hope. "Felicia's getting excellent care. The best there is."

She replied with a bone weary sigh. "I'm so tired. I'm going to tuck myself into bed."

"Rest well."

"Thank you, Seth." She offered him a tender smile that had to be the most beautiful smile in God's great big world. "For everything."

He felt like he'd done very little, yet there was so much more he wanted to give her, to share with her, things they could accomplish together.

Unless he was wrong and his feelings were not hers.

And he'd been wrong before. Dead wrong.

Early the next morning before the sun had officially risen in the storm-clouded sky, Seth joined Levi at the corral fence where he was studying Bubbles.

"Thanks," he said, accepting the mug of coffee Levi handed him.

"How's Nora?"

"Still asleep. She's exhausted, but she's strong, and so is Felicia."

Levi didn't reply.

Seth gestured to Bubbles, who was nosing at some grain. "She close?"

Levi nodded. "Foal will come soon. Udder's swollen. Hindquarters are loosened up. She's restless. Her escapade last night might have sped things up." Levi rubbed his neck. "Nora's good with Bubbles. Getting her to trust in such a short time…that's not easy."

"Yes, she is," he said, feeling a flush of pride that he wasn't entitled to. "Never met a woman like her."

Levi flicked a thumb along his jawline. "She's leaving after the foaling, right?"

He shook his head. "I think she'll stick around until Felicia's situation is resolved. And things are going better with her family, so maybe she'll rent a place in town or something after Felicia's released. Makes sense that she'd want to stay close to them."

He realized Levi was staring at him. "What?"

"Nora's leaving," Levi repeated slowly. "That's what she wants."

"Things change."

Levi cleared his throat. "Sometimes."

Seth read Levi's expression then. Pensive and troubled. "Is there a message coming my way, oh sage cowboy brother?"

"Just saying. If you ride too far ahead of the herd, you might turn around and find it isn't behind you anymore."

"I'm not." His response was defensive, even to his own ears. Was Levi right? Was he rushing ahead imagining reasons for Nora to stay because he desperately wanted her to? His mouth went dry.

Levi slapped his back. "Don't get ahead of yourself is all. Gonna go have some breakfast with Mara if she's feeling up to it. Come with?"

"No, thanks. You go on."

Levi left. Seth stewed. He must be broadcasting the fact that where Nora was concerned, his emotions were at a gallop, or Levi never would have said anything. His quiet friend probably wouldn't again.

Levi cautioned him to maintain the easy friendship trail, to stop running headlong into fields that Nora would never travel. It reminded Seth of what had happened with Tanya. He'd trotted along, imagining their future, woollyheaded with love, only to discover when he turned around he was indeed alone. Levi insinuated he was about to make the same mistake with Nora.

But Levi didn't know Nora like he did. There was still hope.

A pale light in the ranch kitchen window flicked on and Seth imagined Levi making tea for his wife, settling in to share a meal with her. Levi had Mara, Willow loved Tony, and there was Austin and Pilar, Beckett and Laney.

It was his turn to find the love of his life.

To build a family with a one-of-a-kind woman.

A woman he'd begun to imagine was Nora Duke.

He glanced back to the trailer then went into the mini barn. He busied himself cleaning out Bubbles' stall so he wouldn't think of her. The reprieve lasted only minutes until Nora found him.

"Jude called. Felicia is stable and settled in. They've got top-notch security at the Vegas hospital, so she'll be safe." She slid her hands into her pockets. "Looks like I need a place to stay for a while longer, but I don't want to plant myself here if…"

Hope suddenly fountained up inside. She was going to stay for a while. That indicated something, didn't it? "If nothing. You're welcome to the trailer. If you stay until Thursday you'll be here for Christmas Eve." He could not stop the words that spilled out next. "You won't believe the fun we have planned. I can't wait to show you our version of a sleigh ride. After Christmas, Austin and I help Willow out with her star-watching tours. Maybe you can come along. Just the horses, the desert and a million stars. You'll love it."

He finally noticed she was shaking her head. "Seth, I'm sorry," she said apologetically.

"The moment things are cleared up here with Felicia, I'll take Bubbles and her foal and head back to Colorado. My life's there."

At that moment, Levi's wisdom came rushing in.

Yes, Nora was leaving. Yes, he had rushed ahead of her. Yes, he had to accept reality or he would ruin whatever friendship they had. "Right. Sure. I understand."

"But every time I come back, I'd love to catch up."

Catch up. For coffee and a chat. He kept his eyes from rolling. "I get it."

She touched his shoulder. "I can tell you were hoping I'd stay indefinitely, but I told you from the beginning that I wouldn't." Her tone was humiliatingly gentle.

"No, I understand, really," he said, ignoring the cleaver cutting his heart in two. "I sort of hoped you'd changed your mind about that, but it's no big deal."

"My plans haven't changed. They can't, even if there's the chance whoever is a threat might follow me. I've worked too hard to build a future in Colorado. I've got a job there and I'm taking some night classes. I'm going to buy a piece of property when I save up enough. I'll stay a short while, but after that..." She hurried on. "You've been a fantastic friend and I'll never forget it, but…"

"Likewise," he said, forcing his lips to smile. He was good-guy Seth, friend and confidant. And that was all.

"I'll go say hello to Bubbles," Nora said.

He kept the smile in place until she was no longer facing him before he let it die away.

At least it was done now.

No more self-delusion.

Nora would be leaving the ranch and leaving him.

THIRTEEN

Nora had the uneasy feeling she'd hurt Seth. But she'd been perfectly honest since the moment she'd arrived, hadn't she? Her home wasn't in Furnace Falls, in spite of her shakily mended family fences. She had an apartment in Colorado, her work with the donkey rescue. She clung to the belief that Felicia would heal and whoever was after them would be exposed and caught. When that happened, Felicia would restart her life with her mother and perhaps Zane, and Nora would refocus on herself, her work, the next phase of her life. She would be the strong, independent Nora, the woman she wanted to be, and that didn't include a romantic entanglement.

There was no reason to give up what she'd built to return to Death Valley, as wonderful and kind and sweet as Seth was, she told herself. Her heart twisted. She would never reveal that her feelings for him exposed weak and vulnerable places, places she did not want to acknowledge. It was natural to want to get away from that kind of angst, wasn't it?

Yet her soul felt tamped down and burdened as if she'd committed some kind of grievous mistake. As Seth watched from outside the corral, she refocused on Bubbles. The donkey had been exhausted enough to allow herself to be led by a rope the night before and Nora wanted to build on that progress.

With the jenny occupying a corner, Nora simply stood still next to her. Bubbles was less antsy, she thought. Certainly, she did not look worse for wear for her impromptu walkabout. Nora took out a coiled rope she'd stuffed in her back pocket and let the donkey see it. When that didn't provoke undue fear, she touched Bubbles on the side with it. Quick touch, remove, quick touch, remove, until she was able to rest the rope on her neck for several minutes.

When she tried to slip it around Bubbles's neck, the animal flinched. Nora pulled a horse cookie from her pocket. Nostrils quivering, the donkey accepted the treat and the rope, which Nora left on only for a few moments before she removed it.

Progress.

She administered the last injection while Bubbles munched away.

"Time to refill the vitamins with Doc?" Seth said, coming up beside her.

When she nodded, he palmed his keys. "Next stop, vet's office."

His tone was light, but his smile looked forced. *You're imagining things.* He might be mildly disappointed that she wasn't staying, but he had plenty of other things going on. Besides, when she left town, he wouldn't need to worry about protecting her, squiring her around or sleeping on a sofa for guard duty. Much better for everyone.

When they arrived at the veterinary clinic, Jude's squad car was parked outside Doc's office along with another familiar vehicle.

"Zane's here?" Nora's stomach flipped. "What now?"

They entered the office to find Doc flushed and sweating, squared off with Zane. Jude occupied the space between them, his arms raised referee style. Doc's wife, Renee, watched in round-eyed disbelief from the corner, holding the leash of a handsome pointer who was barking madly.

"That's my dog. That's Barney," Zane shouted, stabbing a finger at the pointer. "And Doc's a lousy thief. That's why I called you, Chief."

"Take it down a notch," Jude advised. He

turned to Renee. "Can you put him in the back for a minute?"

She ushered the dog into an exam room, his barking now muted by the door.

"All right. We're going to discuss this calmly," Jude said.

"Why should I?" Zane snapped. "This so-called veterinarian stole my dog. I was driving by and I saw Barney running out of the clinic after him. Otherwise, I never would have known Doc had him." He turned to the vet. "And don't even try to tell me he ran away and you found him. That dog is tagged and you full well knew it was mine."

Nora gaped. Seth looked equally shocked.

"You don't care about these dogs," Doc said, eyes blazing. "You wanted Fred dead anyway."

"Have you lost your wits?" Spot of color highlighted Zane's cheeks. "You're talking nonsense."

"You wanted me to put Fred down for no reason."

"No reason? He became aggressive, remember? Went after me. I fell and busted out my front tooth. Cost me $400 to have that repaired."

Jude stepped closer to Zane. "I will sort this out. Step outside until I'm ready to talk to you."

Zane's hands were fisted at his sides. "Why

should I leave? He's the thief. Bad enough Olivia thinks me and my brother are the dregs in this town. Now I have to be treated like I'm the villain here?"

"Outside," Jude said, volume low but intense. "Now."

Zane stalked out and slammed the door behind him.

"Do you want us to leave too?" Nora asked.

Jude shook his head then gestured them into chairs and pointed to one for Doc, who slumped into it. "No, I need your collective memory for a second. Do you recall that, on the night of the ATV attack, Zane mentioned his dog was missing?"

Nora frowned. "Not really. I was sort of in shock."

"I do," Seth said. "Something about Barney running off. A champion hunting dog or something. Zane said the animal was acting out because his companion had to be euthanized."

"Fred," Doc said. "The other dog's name is Fred."

"Fred and Barney, right." Jude turned to Doc. "Is there something you need to tell me about Fred?"

Doc shrugged, silent.

"Look," Jude said. "We've known each other a long time, Doc, and I'm inclined to believe you had good intent for whatever went down, but you have to tell me the truth. I'm not going to ask twice."

Doc looked at his wife and nodded. She hurried down the hall, opened a door and in a moment another pointer bounded in, went straight to Doc and laid his head on his knee, hind end waggling frantically. Doc stroked the silky muzzle. "Jig's up, Fred. Ole Doc couldn't come through for you." He looked up and blew out a breath, still caressing the dog. "This here's Fred. He's an amazing dog. Not as good a hunting animal as Barney, maybe, but a loyal soul. I've treated him since he and his brother were puppies."

"I'm trying to figure how we got from friendly town vet to dognapper," Jude said.

Not unkindly, Nora thought.

"It's because my husband has a heart of gold," Renee said.

"Don't," Doc said.

"I will say my piece," Renee said, mouth pinched. "Zane brought Fred in and asked Doc to euthanize him. Said he'd become aggressive. We couldn't believe it, but Zane was insistent. Doc tried to talk him out of euthanasia, offered training, and even said we'd take him, but Zane refused. So…" She blinked back tears. "Doc pretended he'd done it and we kept Fred on our property, but the dog loves Doc. It's like he knows Doc saved his life and he escapes the yard and follows Doc everywhere."

Jude nodded. "Okay. So how does Barney fit in?"

Renee jerked a thumb at the exam room. "Barney in there is bonded with Fred."

Doc nodded. "He started running away from the date farm, trying to find Fred. The first time he showed up at our home, I brought him back during the night."

"That's why there were motorcycle tracks on the property."

"Uh-huh, but Barney is a tracking dog. He showed up again the next day at the clinic, barking for Fred. How could I explain that? So I...took him too. Tried to secure them both in my yard, but it was getting ridiculous with all the barking and I thought the neighbors would figure it out, so I began bringing them to work and keeping them in the back. Today I got busted when Zane saw Barney run outside to me." Doc wiped a sleeve over his brow. "It's kind of a relief, actually. All the lying and sneaking around was getting to me."

Jude frowned. "Why do you think Fred bit Zane?"

Doc snorted. "I don't think he did. This here dog's gentle."

"Why would Zane make that up the whole business about his tooth and everything?"

Doc pursed his lips. "I been thinking a lot about that. What if Kai was sneaking around and Fred tried to run him off? I figure either Zane's been covering for his brother and they're involved in something together, or maybe Kai's threatening Zane into keeping secrets. That's the only way I can explain why Zane would destroy a dog he's loved since he was a pup."

"What sort of plot would Zane and his brother be involved in?" Jude said.

"I dunno."

Nora remembered Doc's earlier words. *Blood tells.* Maybe poor Fred had attacked Kai and Zane had to get rid of him.

"All right. I need a few more details. For the moment, I'm going to ask my cousin Austin to take the dogs until there's some clarity here. A neutral party, okay?" When Doc nodded, Jude looked at Nora and Seth. "You two can go."

"Wait," Doc said, retrieving a bag of preloaded syringes for Nora as Fred scuttled alongside as if glued to his ankle. "Bubbles needs her vitamins."

Nora nodded her thanks. Outside, they found Zane leaning against the wall.

"I can't believe he stole my dog," Zane said.

"Wild," Seth agreed. "Why do you suppose Fred became aggressive?"

Zane looked confused. "I don't know. I've always had a way with dogs, but all of a sudden Fred changed."

"He changed? Or was he surprised by a stranger?"

"What's that mean?"

Seth looked straight at him. "Zane, are you covering for your brother?"

Emotion flashed across Zane's face, quickly concealed. Fear? Anger? Resentment? "No, like I told Olivia. Why would I do that?"

"Because you're scared of him," Seth said.

Nora gasped. That was a motive she hadn't thought of. What if Kai was terrorizing Zane into keeping his presence in town a secret? It would explain the dog bite if Zane tried to intervene between Fred and Kai. The dog hadn't attacked his master intentionally, perhaps.

Zane stared back for a moment before he shook his head. "You didn't know my brother. We were opposites in every way. Right-handed versus left-handed. Kai was athletic and I was the brainy one. He loved swimming, I was into climbing. He struggled in school, I aced everything. But in spite of all that, we were close, really close, until he got sent away."

"And then you inherited what he felt was rightfully his," Seth suggested.

Zane shrugged. "He was angry, but that doesn't mean he's some sort of deranged killer."

"Have you had contact with him? You told Olivia you hadn't. Was that the truth?"

"Yes," he said, but Nora noticed he wasn't quite making eye contact until he turned to her. "You messed up years ago, right? You can't escape that in a small town. You caused that crash all those years ago and wrecked Felicia's knee, right?"

A lick of guilt chilled her heart. "Yes, I did."

"But you aren't a bad person. You weren't then and you aren't now. You made mistakes, is all. Same with Kai."

"What happened to Nora and Felicia this week wasn't a mistake," Seth said. "It was attempted murder, and Felicia thought Kai was responsible."

"She was mistaken."

"Felicia said, 'He came back... He'll kill us both,'" Nora said. "Accept it or not, that's your business, but if Kai is behind the attacks on me and Felicia, you have to tell Jude. If Kai's threatening you, Jude can help."

Zane smiled grimly. "Thanks for your concern, but I can take care of myself. I'm real good at it."

Jude opened the door then and gestured Zane into the clinic.

When the men had gone inside, Nora pulled the high school photo from her pocket, since she was no longer comfortable leaving it in the Bronco. Again she examined it.

"Think he's telling the truth?" Seth said, looking over her shoulder.

"I don't know. There's something bugging me, but I can't figure out what." She stared at the photo until her vision blurred. What was the missing piece?

She had to figure it out or neither she nor Felicia would ever be safe.

Seth was locked in a battle in his mind the whole way back to the ranch. Jude kept his word, delivering the dogs to his cousin Austin until the case was sorted out. Seth was undecided. Did he believe Doc or Zane? He never had the chance to decide because as soon as they reached the Rocking Horse corral, Nora gasped.

"Bubbles is in labor," she said as she sprinted from the vehicle to the corral.

He rushed to join her. Bubbles was on her side in the mounded hay. "I'll text Levi," he said.

Nora clutched the fence rail. "I can see the head and front legs of the foal."

Bubbles wriggled and panted and then went limp.

"She can't do it," Nora said. "She's too weak to push the foal out all the way."

Seth checked his phone. "Levi's three miles from here on horseback."

He heard her suck in a breath. "Then it's on us. Are you up to deliver a foal?"

Was he? It was about time to find out. "I'm game if you are."

They approached cautiously. Bubbles struck out her hind hoof to keep them away, but her efforts were half-hearted.

"Steady Bubbles, if you can," Nora said.

Seth applied firm pressure and kept Bubbles as still as he could while Nora freed the foal's head from the placental sack. Seth hadn't been on the ranch long enough to witness any of the horses giving birth. Nerves bubbled up his spine as he tried to soothe the donkey. If things went bad, what were they going to do?

"How do we…?" he started.

The question remained unfinished as Nora seized the emerging donkey's front legs and pulled. "Switch places with me," he said as the effort made her grimace, no doubt from her sore ribs, but Nora did not seem to hear.

She kept pulling steadily until the foal's head and front legs were free. Stopping to catch her breath for only a moment, she grabbed hold of the slippery foal again. "Come on, sweetie," she groaned.

Sweat dampened her forehead. Once she lost her grip and tumbled backward, only to resume her position before he could even move.

"Almost there," she said through clenched teeth.

And then the foal was out, sliding into the clean hay.

Seth gaped at the spindly newborn. He watched with breath held as Nora checked for signs of life. She rubbed it on the muzzle and wiped debris from its nostrils. "Breathing," she said with a sigh of relief. "How's mama?"

Bubbles had flopped down on the hay, eyes closed.

"Exhausted, I think." He stroked her neck. "You did great, Mama Bubbles. Just look at that gorgeous kiddo."

"I'll move her baby closer."

This time he overruled her. "I'm doing it." He gingerly lifted the foal and carried her nearer to Bubbles's head. Nora scraped away some of the sticky straw.

"It's a female, I think." She knelt a few feet

away. "Come on, Mama Bubbles," she whispered. "Say hello to your baby girl."

Seth knelt next to Nora, the scent of straw strong in his nostrils. He could not resist wrapping an arm around her. Together they watched in perfect silence for a few minutes.

"She might be too weak," Nora fretted, worrying her lip between her teeth. He squeezed her shoulder and said a silent prayer for the delicate newborn and her mother. Tears welled in Nora's eyes as she watched them both lying motionless.

"You were incredible," he murmured to Nora. "Fearless and incredible. You did everything you could."

Then Bubbles stirred, opened her eyes and extended her nose to nuzzle her baby, licking and sniffing her.

"Look at that," Nora cried softly. "They're going to be okay." The joy in her voice gave him goose bumps. He looked at her, sweaty, straw stuck in her hair, clothes filthy, and he knew he would never see a more beautiful sight if he lived to be one hundred.

"Thank you, God," he said, voice strangled.

"Yes," Nora agreed. "Thank you, God."

Inching back, they stayed there for a long while, watching the new family. His elation ebbed away as another realization took its place. Since Bubbles had foaled, and Felicia was in Las Vegas, there was no reason for Nora to stay on the ranch much longer.

His spirit dropped, buried under a weight as heavy as a ton of desert sand.

FOURTEEN

Nora stayed near the corral for the rest of the afternoon. She could not get enough of the clumsy foal, who was now standing next to her mother, nursing happily. The sounds of satisfied lip smacking made her giggle. She called her boss to tell him.

"Job well done," he said. "When are you coming back?"

"I'd guess a week or two, if all is well with the donkeys and they're strong enough to travel."

"Super. Any report on Felicia?"

"Holding her own."

"And what about finding out who planted the bomb?"

"No, unfortunately."

He sighed and they ended their conversation.

A week or two? She would be leaving Furnace Falls? Her eyes drifted across the ranch, the lush Christmas tree, Seth stringing yet another set of lights on the fence while keeping a close eye on her. The tantalizing notion of spending Christmas on the ranch flitted across her brain. But if she stayed, she'd be drawn further into the festivities, pulled ever closer to Seth.

The longer she remained at the Rocking Horse, the harder it would be to go. Every day she felt herself becoming more and more attached to him, which would force her to consider a future in Furnace Falls. The place she'd turned away from; the town where she'd committed colossal mistakes. The image of a homey Christmas, like some sort of Normal Rockwell painting, evaporated.

She was not Sadie Nora Duke anymore. She was Nora, and she certainly didn't want to embrace a town where her sins would be forever remembered. God forgave, she understood that now, but small-town folks didn't. What had Zane said? *You messed up years ago. You can't escape that in a small town.* That was why she'd left in the first place.

The real problem was that caring about Seth made her vulnerable. It softened her heart, eased her defenses, left her too relaxed and she lost touch with reality.

She saw Seth jump as he whacked his thumb with a hammer. Sheepishly, he sucked it and cut a look at her, that comical, self-deprecating expression he so often displayed. He made her laugh. He took impeccable care of her, yet she knew he had his own inner scars from a woman who'd hurt him. Seth deserved a nice local girl who hadn't burned her bridges, not someone with a trail of wreckage and walls of prickles around her heart. Pain settled beneath her ribs. He could be a man who made her want to stay, to rebuild permanently what she'd left in ruins.

But he hadn't asked her to.

And she hadn't offered. She didn't have the courage to be that vulnerable.

Time to go, she told herself as she returned to the trailer near sunset. Right now. Better to make her exit quick and painless. Resolutely, she packed her bag.

Seth arrived with steaming bowls of soup as the sun set and the Christmas tree blazed to life against the darkness.

"Corinne is attempting to bake Christmas cookies with Willow and Mara," he said. "They asked if you wanted to join in. I—" He saw her duffel bag. "Are you leaving?"

"Not the area, but I'm giving you the trailer back. You might need it over the holidays. I found a room for rent right across the street from Austin and Pilar's. Jude already put Austin on alert that he's my new babysitter."

Seth frowned. "I never thought of myself as your babysitter."

She forced a laugh. "I didn't either, but now you can return to your regularly scheduled life. I'll come back and forth to care for the donkeys until they're well enough to travel." Her nerves went all jumpy. *Don't say anything else, Seth. Let's walk away without any further awkwardness. It's better for both of us.*

He set the bowls on the table and looked at her, grave and thoughtful.

Would he try to argue her out of her decision?

"Okay. I can see you've made up your mind," he said.

With a dull ache, she realized her prickles had finally succeeded in keeping him away. Whatever they might have had was no longer even a possibility. Just like she'd intended, like she wanted. She'd made the right decision to leave the ranch.

A popping sound grabbed their attention. Seth ran to the window and heaved a sigh of relief. "It's the tree. It just went dark. We must have blown a line or something. I—" And then the spark of light turned into a ball of orange flame.

"Fire!" they both said at once.

"Stay here. I'll be back." He said the words as he was bolting out the trailer door.

She stood on the porch, watching Seth run through the night. Levi came barreling out of the house with a barking Banjo behind him. The men shouted commands as they rushed for the extinguishers. She hoped they'd get the flames out quickly before the fire destroyed the beautiful tree that had enchanted Corinne's young son.

And you, Nora.

Truth be told, she *had* savored the sight of the Christmas tree and all it represented. Family. Faith. The future. Sadness crept over her again and she closed her eyes to forestall any tears.

When she opened them, she saw a figure in the darkness, leaping onto the porch. She felt a vicious shove and she was driven back into the trailer. Her head slammed into the floor and she saw stars as the door shut with a thump.

Kai? she thought, struggling to scream, but her attacker pressed a beefy palm over her mouth.

He dropped to a knee next to her, breath hot on her face. Kai? Or Zane? Her vision was too blurred. Her thoughts twined together and a realization exploded in her consciousness like a bomb as she recalled the snippets of conversation.

We were opposites in every way. Right-handed versus left-handed, Zane had said, defending his brother.

Or so she'd thought.

But she'd been wrong. Dead wrong.

Her skin crawled at the enormity of her mistake. Though the familiar man in front of her was beardless, the hand pressed over her mouth was his *left* one. The humble date farmer she'd interacted with upon returning to Furnace Falls was *left-handed*, but the high school photos of the set painting and the mini golf was visual proof that the real Zane was right-handed. This wasn't Zane. It was Kai.

Felicia must have suspected something was wrong. She would have before anyone else, of course, since she'd been infatuated with Zane back in high school. She'd probably begun to realize certain things didn't add up with the boyfriend she'd remembered.

He'd said it himself the night of the ATV attack, which she realized now he was responsible for. *I've been having a laugh looking through our old yearbook like you suggested. Can't believe we were ever so young. It's like looking at somebody else's life.*

It was the literal truth. The man they believed was Zane Freeman was actually his brother Kai.

He looked at her and smiled. "I can tell you figured it out. Something in the photos told you, right? Something I let slip to Felicia? Matter of time before she realized I wasn't her old boyfriend." He sighed. "She wanted so badly to rekindle the high school flame with Zane that she was happy to blame everything on bad seed Kai, so I decided to help that idea along. Why not? If everyone thought bad brother Kai was lurking around, responsible for attempted murder, no one would look at me. I could kill Felicia, you, and the cops would still be following a red herring."

Nora felt dizzy as the pieces fell into place. *My brother's not a bad guy...* The constant defense not of his brother, but of himself. It had been so convincing.

The way the dog Fred became a biter, not because the animal changed, because Zane had. Fred knew his master was gone, suddenly replaced by a stranger.

"If you two hadn't come to town, I could have lived as Zane without anyone ever knowing, most likely." Kai wrapped a strip of duct tape over her mouth then around her wrists and ankles. "I'm going to hope that Felicia never comes out of that coma, but if she does, she'll be in the hospital for a while, so that'll give me time to deal with her. One way or another, she'll never live long enough to be a problem." He squeezed her shoulders so hard it drew tears. "I am going to get the life I deserve. That's all I ever wanted. The farm, the money…it all should have been mine from the start, but Zane convinced Mom to give him the property. If you'd opened the letter bomb, that would have sped things up, but I'm okay with altering the plan."

Nora tried to control the panic. She stopped gasping and focused on breathing through her nose. She told herself Seth was right across the ranch at the main house. If she could make noise, attract his attention…

"Now," Kai said, grabbing the keys to her truck from the wall peg. "We're gonna send Seth a text as soon as we get away from here." He flicked a look at her duffel. "Handy that you're already packed. They'll be busy for a while with the tree since there's another mini explosion about to happen which will amp up the fire."

Of course the fire was no accident. Kai was again demonstrating his prowess with demolitions.

Cautiously, he opened the trailer door and she scooted over, trying to hook her foot around a chair leg and send it crashing down. He turned in time, caught the chair and hauled her up by her bound hands. As he dragged her to the truck, she fought and kicked, but it did no good, especially with her hands bound behind her. He shoved her in and reached for the ignition.

The engine noise, she thought. Surely it would cause Seth to look over. He'd come and save her.

Kai studied at his watch. "Three, two, one..." He put up his index finger with a grin. Another small pop pierced the night as Kai's second explosive went off and a new section of the tree caught fire, covering the sound of the motor when he turned the key.

Kai drove with the lights off, down the road, away from the ranch. Every moment lessened her chance for escape, took her farther away from any kind of help.

She tried to wriggle enough to sit up. Then she could attempt to reach the door handle and jump out. Maybe a passerby would see her. But as soon as they were clear of the road, far enough away that no one at the ranch would see, Kai stopped. As the engine idled, he pulled the phone from her pocket and typed.

Hey, Seth. Last-minute change. I decided to drive up and visit Felicia. Staying overnight in Las Vegas. Can you check on the burrow for me?

He narrated as he typed then shoved the phone up to her face. "How's it look? Okay?"

She did not prompt him to correct his misspelling of burro. She merely stared at him, fear and anger boiling inside.

"Awww, someone's in a bad mood?" He pressed Send and pocketed her phone. "I get it. We're not so different, you and me. You left everything behind, so you're an outsider too. Small-town people can be narrow-minded. Holding on to grudges forever, am I right?"

Nora squirmed, her fingers searching for the door handle. Run, hop, roll, flail. She'd do whatever it took to get away from Kai. Before she could make a move, he pulled a plastic bag from his pocket, opened it, and shoved it under her nose. She fought not to inhale but the fumes stung and she felt her body begin to go numb.

Frantically, she writhed, banging her head on the side of the truck.

"Nighty night, Nora," Kai said. "You and Felicia never should have come back to Furnace Falls."

As the edges of Nora's vision began to dim, a thought poked at her.

Never should have come back.

Small towns, unforgiving people. For ten years she'd thought the same, but now she had the terrible realization that the person who couldn't let go of the past was herself. And now it was too late. Unable to hold her breath any longer, she gasped in some tainted air. One question hit her as she lost consciousness.

If Kai had assumed his brother's identity... then where was Zane?

Seth blasted the burning pine needles with another spray of foam from the extinguisher when the branch above it popped and caught fire. "This is wild," he said as he and Levi beat back the flames. Mara looked on, hand on the phone to call in the emergency in case the fire threatened the house. Fortunately, the recent rains had left the needles fairly damp, so it was an easier job to put out the flames than it might have been.

He'd emptied the extinguisher when his phone rang.

"Seth, something's not right." It was Jude.

"You're telling me." He was about to explain the tree fire when Jude continued.

"It didn't feel logical to me that Fred suddenly attacked his owner."

Seth went still. "Uh-huh. I didn't think so either."

"Remember that stuff about Zane's broken tooth?"

"Yes."

"Can't exactly ignore a broken front tooth, right?"

"Right. Where are you going with this?"

"I talked to Doctor Bev."

Bev Reynolds was the only dentist in Furnace Falls and she'd enjoyed a thirty-year practice to date. Seth waited, nerves prickling.

"She didn't treat him," Jude said.

"Why not?"

"Oh, he called her, that part checked out, but he asked her for an out-of-town referral. Said he had to make a trip and he couldn't take the time to get it fixed first."

"What's your take, Jude?" Seth said, his pulse slowly accelerating.

"In my business, teeth are a big deal, right? Sometimes they're the only proof of a person's identity." He paused. "It's a theory, of course, but I'm thinking why wouldn't Zane want the local dentist to fix his teeth?"

His grip tightened on the phone. "Because the local dentist would realize her patient wasn't Zane Freeman. The dental records wouldn't match."

"That's what I came up with too."

Seth's gaze traveled over the blackened tree. What if the tree fire was not an accident? Kai knew all about explosives. "So the guy we know as Zane is actually…"

"Kai."

"Jude, Kai's after Nora," Seth clenched the phone and sprinted toward the trailer.

"Her truck's missing," he yelled to Jude as he pounded through the unlocked trailer door with his blood surging.

Fear turned into ice-cold terror.

Nora was gone.

Nora didn't know how long it had been since she'd drifted in and out of consciousness. When she finally blinked awake, confusion muddled her senses. It took her a moment to realize her heels were bumping and scraping over gritty ground. Dragged! She was being dragged. Struggling earned her a violent shake and Kai snarled in her ear.

"Don't slow us down. It's only going to hurt more if you fight."

It all rushed back to her and she twisted in his grasp, but her hands were still taped behind, her mouth sealed shut. The ground flashing in front of her eyes became rocky, twisted shrubs pulling at her hair and clawing her clothes.

"Almost there," he said. "Let me lay this out for you. You're going to have an accident on your way to visit Felicia, but timing is important. I think Jude suspects I'm not being honest, especially now that Doc's turned traitor, so he might come looking if he doesn't believe the text. I'm going to keep you here for a few hours, long enough to let him search around if he wants to. I will assist him in any way possible, of course.

"When all is quiet, we'll head out. There's a real nice secluded road between here and Las Vegas. You're going to get lost, disoriented, turn down that road and wham, before you know it, you're dead in a tragic accident. Might take them a long time to find your body, but don't worry. I'll help with the search. Zane Freeman is nothing if not an upstanding guy."

The chloroform had left her groggy with a pounding headache but the cool air was reviving her somewhat. *Breathe and focus*, she told herself. She was strong, determined. All she needed was a few more minutes to shake off the effects of her drugging.

But suddenly he stopped walking.

Her shoes impacted a rocky ledge and a waft of dank air hit her nostrils.

"What are you doing with me?" she wanted to shout.

"I've got a ladder hidden here for later when

I want to get you out so we can hit the road. But for now…"

He dragged her to her feet and put a palm on her back. With a sudden push, he shoved her over the edge. Screaming in silence, she tumbled into the dark shaft.

FIFTEEN

"I'll get help," Levi announced when he caught up, after there was no reply to multiple calls and texts to Nora's phone. "We'll canvas the town. There's a possibility we're wrong and the text was legit, maybe Nora stopped for gas or water."

Mara had already called Aunt Kitty in case Nora had contacted her. She hadn't, and since Kitty was clearly worried, she'd driven over to stay with her.

It was all conjecture at this point. The timing of the tree fire and Nora's departure might be a coincidence. They had no real proof that Kai had assumed Zane's identity, but Seth felt in his bones that Jude was right.

Seth tried to give equal weight to the alternative scenario. What if he was wrong and she'd just decided to move up her departure? Because of him? *Wearing your feelings on your sleeve, again?* She was planning on moving out of the trailer the next day, so wasn't it possible she'd merely left earlier? But Bubbles and her yet unnamed foal hadn't been bedded down for the night and Nora wasn't the kind to leave her chores to someone else, no matter what the circumstances.

He fell back on that well of intuition that he'd relied on so heavily in his medic days. What did his gut say?

Something is wrong and Kai's behind it.

If Kai had taken Zane's identity, it explained so much. Seth ran through the timeline.

Felicia knew Zane well. She was close enough to find out the truth, so she posed a threat.

Kai staged the ATV attack and showed up as Zane, appearing concerned. Felicia might have suspected later that it was Kai's doing, providing the perfect way to throw suspicion off the man who'd stolen his brother's identity.

Kai continued the charade and pretended someone was watching, having already left the binoculars where he would appear to find them.

He wore a fake beard to make sure Nora identified Kai before he stole the photos that he feared might incriminate him. Worried Nora might stumble upon his real identity, he tried to corner her in the wash, left the letter bomb where she'd touch it.

Seth recalled snippets of Doc's confession. How he questioned why Zane would destroy a dog he'd loved since he was a pup. The answer was that Zane wouldn't. But Kai would.

The whole thing was genius really. Kai became his brother, took his assets, but used his real-life tarnished reputation to divert suspicion.

And Seth had played right into Kai's hands by rushing off to fight the tree fire.

Without a word, Seth climbed in next to Jude in the squad car the second he arrived.

"What's your take?" Jude demanded as he threw the car in gear.

"She wouldn't have misspelled 'burro' in her text."

"A misspelled word isn't proof…but I'm inclined to agree. Nora won the middle school spelling bee two years in a row." He gunned the engine down the road from the ranch. "We don't have a warrant to search the date farm, so unless I see some kind of indication he's taken her, I can't do anything without his permission."

"I can. I'm going to tear apart every square inch of that property until I'm satisfied she's not there."

"Can't let you do that. You'll mess up any case we might have."

"I don't care about the case. All I care about is Nora."

Jude's jaw clenched. "You don't think I'm worried too, Seth? She's my sister. How would you feel if it was Mara or Corinne we were talking about?"

Seth heard Jude's teeth grind together. He breathed himself into a calmer tone. "I'm sorry. Nora's very important to both of us."

Jude shot him a side-eye. "How important?"

Seth tried unsuccessfully to come up with a reply as they headed for the date farm.

"Speechless, huh?" Jude said. "All right. If we get her out of trouble, you're going to be sure to come up with something better than awkward silence, right?"

He blew out a breath. "She doesn't want to stick around. She's been clear on that score."

"A stubborn Duke? Imagine that," Jude said. "She's got baggage, or haven't you been paying attention? But she's a Duke and, at the end of the day, she knows her roots are here and maybe even her future if she came to believe someone loved her enough to make her let go of all the past wreckage."

Seth's heart ached. He could not deny that he loved her madly, truly, completely. "I'm not sure she thinks I'm that guy," he said after a moment.

"Then you'd better get busy," Jude snapped.

They careened on, lost in their own thoughts, until Jude rolled to a stop before the bridge to the Freeman date farm, engine idling. "All right. I'm going to go talk to him and, unless I get a real innocent vibe or hear that Nora's been located elsewhere, I'm getting back in my vehicle and securing a search warrant and more officers."

Seth reached for the door handle, realizing he hadn't brought his rifle along. Probably for the best, since Kai was still technically innocent. *Innocent, my aching shoulder.* "I'll keep to the public land, circle around and see if I can spot her vehicle or any clue that he's got her. I'll text you either way."

Jude grabbed his shoulder in a painful squeeze. "Seth, you're not a cop and we have no rights here."

"I got all that earlier." Seth tried to pull away but Jude only tightened his grip.

"If Zane is actually Kai, he's got everything to lose and he won't hesitate to kill you. You see anything at all, you text and wait. Don't go all cowboy on me."

"Cuz I'm not a Duke?"

"Because you're not a cop," Jude said firmly. "And I don't want you hurt."

Been there, done that, Seth thought as he

nodded and got out. He'd faced his injury and agonizing rehabilitation and what's more, he'd accepted that he was not the man he used to be. But God kept him alive and kicking, and he would use up every ounce of that gift to find Nora.

Seth closed the car door quietly and slipped off the gravel road into the thicket. The pine needles dripped icy moisture as he ran along the river, paralleling the embankment where Nora had plunged when she'd staged her ambush during the ATV attack. He could see her in his memory, arms folded, hair streaming, jackknifing into the ice-cold water. And he remembered his own gut reaction. Awe and admiration. Since then, those twin sensations had only strengthened.

A woman like that would fight to her last bit of courage, he told himself. And if she hadn't? If she was already dead?

He shoved the fear away and pushed himself to go faster. His arm was beginning to tremble, already stressed by his efforts to extinguish the fire. As he hunched down and kept to the trees, he visualized Nora, her energetic stride, the way her laugh seemed too big for her slender frame. He thought of the first time he'd seen her on Zoom and the way he'd gone all cold and hot and nervous and relaxed at the same time. The message screamed through his nerve pathways and pierced his heart like an arrow.

I love her. Lord, if she needs saving, give me the strength and let me be enough.

He ran on into the night.

Cold. Damp. The tang of mildew. Sensations assailed Nora's senses as she swam back to consciousness.

When she'd hit the bottom of the shaft, the impact had left her stunned. She didn't know how long she'd lain crumpled there, struggling to get oxygen in. Dull pain radiated through her side along with a rising sense of chill.

Breathe, just breathe.

When she was able to get her lungs to cooperate, she slowly sat up.

I can't see, she thought with a flutter of sheer terror, until she looked up and discerned a vague light some fifteen feet above her. Faint moonlight, she realized. Behind her back, her bound fingers grazed a rotting wood beam and rough rock. She was in some sort of shaft, she realized. Not surprising. Death Valley was a labyrinth of underground mining tunnels.

The bottom of the shaft was covered with piles of leaves, dirt, stones and who knew what else.

Rocks stabbed into her hips. *All right. First*

thing's first. She scooted back and forth until she felt a particularly sharp rock poking at her. Ignoring the pain in her shoulders, she worked her wrists back and forth over that roughness, sawing at the tape. Sweat poured down her face, chilling her further, and she had to stop several times to ease the agony in her muscles. At long last, she was rewarded when the tape gave way.

Gasping, she ripped the pieces off and chafed life back into her bruised wrists before she peeled the tape off her mouth and ankles.

Elated, she wriggled her feet to restore the circulation. Clinging to the beam for support, she hauled herself up. Dizziness swamped her but she locked her knees until it passed. Head injury or the results of being drugged, she wasn't sure, but it didn't matter. She had to get out of that shaft before Kai returned.

She wondered if Seth would ever realize what had actually happened to her.

What would he think when he got her text? Would he believe she'd decided to up and leave town so abruptly?

It was entirely possible since she'd rebuffed him. Why had she been such a fool?

No time for that now, she told herself savagely. There had to be a way out of this shaft. She took a step and collapsed in pain. Her ankle was damaged, broken maybe. Well, it wasn't going to stop her from climbing out.

Measured breathing controlled the discomfort as she carefully got to her feet, putting her weight slowly on her uninjured leg. Then she set about patting her hands along the grimy walls. The shaft was some ten feet across, she estimated, with a generous eighteen inches of detritus on the bottom. Perhaps there was an old pipe or a series of rocks placed in such a way that she could climb out. She wished she had her phone flashlight. The moon did little more than paint the shaft in lighter tones of gray.

Would Jude actually stop at the date farm to look for her as Kai expected? If he did, would he be convinced by Kai's innocent act? That was a factor she couldn't control, so she did what came naturally now. She prayed.

When she finished, she hopped on one foot through the debris. Maybe there was something she could use down there, a discarded rope or cable. Unlikely, but she was going to explore every minute possibility.

As she staggered on her injured ankle, she thought again of what Kai had said. *You left everything behind, so you're an outsider... Small-town people can be narrow-minded. Holding on to grudges forever..."*

Yes, Olivia was still angry, but Nora discovered that her brother, her mother, the Dukes, they were all willing to forgive, if she had only decided to let them. Her own stubbornness made her cringe. If she didn't get out of that shaft, her realization wouldn't amount to a hill of beans.

A hill…she thought. If there were rocks buried in the debris, maybe she could pile them up and reach high enough to grab hold of the ledge of rock she could barely make out above her head. It wouldn't boost her enough to get out, but maybe it would show her another set of rocks or a jutting piece of wood that could lead the way to the next handhold.

Dropping to her knees, she pushed her palms through the rotting leaves. The vegetation felt as clammy as eels. Her fingertips encountered a piece of wedge-shaped wood or rubber. There was something familiar about it that her brain would not at first accept.

What was it?

Trailing her fingers along, she felt the material, both rigid and supple.

Leather.

The hard-tooled leather of a cowboy boot.

Not a cowboy's boot, a farmer's.

She understood now what Kai had done with his brother.

Her scream echoed back at her.

SIXTEEN

Seth walked for what seemed like hours until his phone pinged.

Spotted nothing overt, **Jude messaged,** but Farmer Zane couldn't explain why there's fresh oil drops on his driveway and yet his truck engine's cold. With a warrant, I can check in the barn and outbuildings for Nora's vehicle. Calling for one now and I'm watching the house. Report?

Nothing, Seth reluctantly texted back.

And that's when he noticed a rut in the soft earth outside the gate to the property. He shone his phone light over the ground, but there was no sign of any other disturbance. His imagination? Or perhaps other marks had been brushed away? A light rain had begun to fall, muddying the ground.

Checking something, Seth texted.

What? Jude demanded immediately, but instead of replying, Seth used the light, shielded by his cupped fingers. It was a gouge in the earth, as if something substantial might have been dragged along. He decided to walk west, away from the gate, and he texted Jude, but the swirling "sending" dots indicated he was in a dead zone. Should he go back and report to Jude or keep going?

Urgency drove him forward. A few broken branches begged him to come closer and he pushed through, wet leaves splatting his forehead.

"Nora?" he whispered. Had he heard something or was it the hammering of his heart against his rib cage? "Nora?" he called again.

A faint reply, high-pitched and quavering, made his whole body prickle. "Down here."

"Nora," he shouted now, plunging into the bushes, heedless of the grasping branches. He almost fell into the hole nearly concealed by a lip of jutting rocks. Catching himself, he crashed to his knees and shoved his head into the opening. "Are you down there?"

Maybe he wanted it so badly his mind was supplying what he wanted to believe. How could it actually be her? He shone his light into what appeared to be a bottomless rocky chute, the flicker unable to penetrate the darkness.

But the word that drifted up to his straining ears lit him up like the brightest torch.

"Seth."

Swamped with relief, he shoved his head and shoulders in as far as he dared. "I'm going to get you out."

"There's a ladder hidden somewhere up there."

A ladder? He tore himself away and prowled the bushes, checking again to see if he had a signal. More twirling dots, but he sent the text to Jude anyway. His boot whacked into the bottom rung of a ladder lying flat on the ground underneath the bushes.

Muscles quivering, he dragged it free and lugged it to the edge of the shaft. It took some time and maneuvering, but he lowered the unwieldy thing into the darkness.

He heard her cry of pain. "What's wrong?"

"I hurt my ankle," Nora said. "I don't think I can't climb up."

"Then I'm coming down to get you," he said, even as he was tackling the first few rungs. His arm and upper thigh were tremoring but he pushed that from his mind. *Get to Nora. Get her out.* The words played a deafening drumbeat in his mind.

He hit the bottom rung and stepped into a pile of squishy debris. Whirling, heart beating as if it would explode, he turned and found her. His Nora, he thought as he embraced her.

She leaned against him, choking with sobs, her body quaking.

"It's okay now. We're going to get out of here."

"Zane…" she half whispered, half sobbed. She could not say the rest, so he shined a light in the direction she pointed.

Seth saw the booted foot protruding from the mess of debris. He stifled a groan. "Kai will pay for what he's done to his brother. But right now, we need to get out of here."

She wiped her eyes with the heels of her hands. "No argument, but…" She tried again to put weight on her ankle. The pain made her unable to sustain it. Climbing would be out of the question.

"No problem. Hold on to my waist."

She did and they made it a few rungs up before Seth's compromised side began to give out. He continued on doggedly, his limbs heating with the effort, but he knew he would not make it. He had no choice but to return them to the bottom. Distraught, he tried again to send a text with no result. He had no idea if Jude had gotten his last texts.

There had to be a way to get out of the shaft. Why would God have brought him so far only to leave him unable to get Nora out?

To get his attention, she touched his cheek,

her fingertips freezing cold. He caught them between his palms, desperate to warm her. "Just need to rest a minute," he said.

She shook her head. "No you don't. It's too much, dragging both of us."

"Nora," he said through gritted teeth. "I'm not giving up until you're safe and out of here. Understand?"

"Yes," she said with the barest gleam of a smile. "But I was thinking, you've got an injured right side and I've got a tweaked left ankle. That means between us, we should be able to rustle up all the arms and legs we need."

"What?"

"Can I have a piggyback ride? I'll be your right arm and you can be my left leg."

He gaped. He would have believed her to be joking, if he didn't hear the determination in her voice. "Let's get out of here, Seth. Together. It's the only way."

Together. How he loved the sound of it. She climbed onto his back, looped her arm around his neck and held on. Together he hauled them up one step, holding on with his good hand and Nora clasping the rung tightly with hers. Awkwardly, ungracefully, with excruciating effort, they advanced up the rungs.

The top one was the hardest since they were both exhausted.

"Let go and climb out," Seth commanded.

"Together," Nora panted.

"This is the finish line, Nora. You cross first."

"No."

"Allow me to be a gentleman here," he rasped. "Ladies first."

With a sigh, she climbed out, immediately turning around on her knees to grip his arm as he tried to follow suit. His muscles were at their limit but Nora tugged for all she was worth and Seth managed to crawl from the shaft. They knelt together, gasping for breath, but only for a few seconds.

He was struggling to his feet when a shot blasted over his head. With his last strength, he pulled Nora behind him and rose to face their attacker.

Nora read the desperation on Kai's face and in the way he gripped the shotgun. He shook his head. "All right. Plan B. I'm not going to jail, do you hear me? Zane got what he deserved and I'm not going down for that."

Seth did not move from his position in front of her. "Jude's here."

"I know. I snuck out the back door. I only need a few minutes."

"It's over," Seth said quietly. "You can't get away."

Kai shrugged. "Guess hostages are my only option now. But I only need one," he said. "So looks like Seth dies."

"No," Nora shouted.

Kai took aim anyway.

"Get down, Nora," Seth said as he dove for Kai.

Both Kai and Seth tumbled to the ground.

Nora was too terrified to scream, to move. She stumbled, collapsing on her bad ankle, crawling toward Seth, trying to grab for a rock or tree limb she could use as a weapon.

Seth rolled over and delivered a punishing punch to Kai's chin. He went limp and still just as Jude stepped out of the brush, revolver gripped in both hands. "Move back, Nora. Now."

Nora did, her blood still iced with fear.

Seth rolled over and worked to get his knees underneath him. Kai lay on his back, groaning, blood trickling from his mouth.

Jude edged forward and kicked the shotgun out of reach. Seth rolled to his feet and checked Kai's pulse. "Ambulance?" he said.

"Rolling." Jude grinned. "Not bad for a contractor turned cowboy."

Seth's gaze went to Nora. The question was silent, the same one mirrored in Jude's quick glances.

Are you all right?

It took all her energy to nod.

Jude was still watching Kai but he flicked a glance at her.

"Sis?" he said.

I'm safe, thanks to Seth, and you. Those were the words she wanted to say.

But the only thing that came out of her mouth was a muffled sob. She thanked God from the depths of her soul as Seth took her in his arms.

On Christmas Eve two days later, Nora finished packing and tidying up the trailer. She wandered out to the corral, limping slightly. Bubbles and her little one, whom Seth had insisted should be called Pinky for the pink splotch on her muzzle, stood like silver statues in the moonlight. Nora's heart was full as she watched the leggy foal nurse from her mother. She didn't think she had room for more joy, since she'd also heard that Felicia was out of her coma, though she'd have a long road to full recovery, but the donkey duo lifted her spirit.

Felicia would need to be told about Zane, but not just yet, not while she was still so fragile. Olivia had begun to text updates, which was also an encouraging sign. Maybe since she'd heard that Kai was behind the attacks, she'd moved Nora out of the enemy camp.

A car pulled up and Jude hopped out, opening the passenger door for their mother. He gave her his arm and she walked painfully to join Nora at the corral fence.

"She insisted on seeing the new addition," Jude said.

Kitty cooed and admired the donkey baby for a moment before turning to Nora. "The foal is adorable, as expected, but actually, I wanted to see you. What do you think of my offer?"

Nora took a deep breath. "I would be honored to come home for a while. My room could use a good tidying up."

Kitty enveloped her in a hug. Jude smiled and wrapped his arms around both of them. "About time my two favorite women were back together." He gave Nora a squeeze. "Missed you, sis," he whispered in her ear.

"Ditto," she said, choking back the emotion. The magnitude of what God had done in her life robbed her of speech for a moment.

"Joining us for Christmas Eve dinner?" Kitty said, pointing to the bedecked tables outside the main house where a firepit cast a soft glow over the whole scene. "Afterwards we go to the late service at the church. It's so beautiful with the lanterns and holly everywhere." She swallowed, eyes brimming. "It will be even more beautiful this year."

And Seth would be there, too, no doubt, with his whole family. The man had saved her life, but out of her stubbornness and fear, she'd made it clear she didn't want a relationship with him. She'd served up a rejection, like Tanya had. And it had hurt him, hurt them both.

"I…" She turned to see Seth approaching, dressed in black jeans and a neat button-up shirt.

"Come on, Mom," Jude said. "I'll drive you closer to the house."

Kitty allowed herself to be led to the car. They drove slowly away.

Nerves danced in Nora's stomach as Seth drew near. What should she say? And how?

"I, uh, did I hear right? That you're going to stay with your mom?" Seth said.

"For a while. Not long term."

"Ah. Right." His expression was troubled, though he hid it behind a slight smile. She knew him well enough after what they'd been through.

And you know yourself now too. So what's it going to be, Nora?

She brushed her hair back from her brow. "I was thinking about what I said before." She fought back a ripple of panic and rushed on. "When I told you I had no reason to stay in Furnace Falls."

He nodded. "I remember."

Courage, Lord. Give me courage. "I saw hurt in your eyes. Am I right about that?"

Now he looked at her curiously. "Yes," he said after a beat.

"That made me think you…" She inhaled deeply. "That you had feelings for me." Time ticked to a stop. "Did I get it wrong, Seth?" She sought the answer in his green eyes but the darkness shadowed them.

"No," he said slowly. "You didn't. But it's not just regular feelings." He rested his forearms on the fencing. "I'm no good at lying, Nora. I fell in love with you."

Hope surged in her chest, prickling her skin with goose bumps. "You did?" Fell? Past tense?

He sighed. "Yes, but I'm not going to stand in the way of what's best for you. You don't want to be here, making a future with me. You said as much."

The fear of baring her soul made her go cold, but she took his hand, his fingers twining with hers as if they belonged that way. "I was wrong."

He stared at their joined hands. "Wrong?" He blinked. "I feel like I'm trying to eat a soup sandwich here. You made it clear. You needed my help but you didn't want anything more."

She shook her head. "I thought I wanted space and freedom and to blot out what happened here in Furnace Falls, but what I really needed was to forgive myself. God let me do that and, what's more, He helped me understand I wanted the wrong thing. And now He's giving me the courage to be completely honest with you."

Bubbles whinnied softly but Seth didn't turn his head. He was stock-still, as if he was afraid to move an inch. "And what's that, Nora?" he murmured. "What do you want?"

Her whole body went suddenly shivery. This was the moment. She could risk everything or make an excuse and walk away. "The reconciliation with my family…"

He smiled. "Check that one off the list."

She forced out a breath. "I want a man I can love without limits."

He opened his mouth to speak but remained silent.

She rushed on. "I want and need a life partner, a faith partner, a man who isn't afraid to be who he is, gentle, kind, strong and steady, and accepts me for who I am, a thistle, prickly with a tender middle." She inhaled deeply. "What I want and need is you."

He stared. "Am I dreaming this?"

"Not unless I'm dreaming it with you." She pulled him away from the rail and traced a finger down his cheek. "I love you, Seth."

He faced her full-on, but she wasn't sure if she read shock or happiness in his expression. He pulled his mouth tight and tipped his gaze to the moon. She waited, feeling as if her heart had stopped.

"I fell in love with you over a computer screen," he said, his voice husky, "and all that's happened here has only cemented that. I thought it was not going to happen, that you'd leave and I'd try to forget the way you made my life better just by being in it." He dropped his gaze to hers. "I love you, Nora Duke. And I will love you until God takes us home."

He sank down onto his knee. "If you'll be my wife, I can promise a life of laughter and love and lots of bumbling on my part." His voice quavered. "I've got no ring to offer right now but…"

She laughed, a peal of happiness that went right up into the night. "I don't need a ring, Seth. I just need you," she whispered.

He jumped up, his arms went around her and her limbs trembled with the sheer pleasure of it. Seth was hers and she was his. He hugged her and swung her around as the donkeys watched, fascinated.

"There's only one thing left to do," he said, eyes damp with tears as he set her gently down.

"What's that?"

"I'll tell you on the sleigh ride."

"A sleigh ride? In the desert?"

He grinned and kissed her. "You just wait, Nora Duke. The desert is full of surprises and so am I."

Seth was still brimming with overwhelming happiness as he led the horses along. They were hitched to an old-fashioned sleigh that glided easily over the sandy path from the barn. They laid extra sand every year to ensure an easy trip for the horses. The route brought them by the corral on the way to the ranch house Christmas tree. Beckett and Austin had worked tirelessly to haul in a new tree and affix fresh ornaments and lights. It glittered in full glory as Seth guided the sleigh. The scent of bubbling stew and warm biscuits made his mouth water. The selection of Christmas pies would wait until after church.

He could hardly bear to let go of Nora's hand, so he settled for having her sit next to him, holding the cluster of thistles he'd snagged earlier and wrapped in his scarf. In the back seat, Corinne held on to Peter, who was electric with excitement. Next year Mara and Levi would add their new baby to the proceedings.

Life was good. God was good. Seth knew he'd been blessed beyond imagining.

"I can't believe I'm on a sleigh ride in the desert," Nora said.

"There's nothing better than a Death Valley Christmas," Corinne piped up.

Bubbles and Pinky watched the pageant with curiosity as the sleigh jingled toward their destination. The family was assembled at the tables. He felt like a kid on Christmas morning as he pulled the sleigh to a stop at the Christmas tree.

"I have an announcement to make," he said to the group clustered with mugs of cider at the ready.

"Have you finally finished remodeling the trailer?" Levi joked.

"Nah," Jude put in. "He'll be working on that until he's ninety at least."

"Pipe down, you unruly Dukes." Seth pulled Nora up from her seat. "Nora and I are officially engaged," he said.

There was a collective cheer. Jude's whoop of enthusiasm was loudest of all. Kitty's face was streaked with tears.

"Nora's going to live with Aunt Kitty while we plan the shindig and she works on her idea to start a donkey sanctuary right here in Furnace Falls, but I want you to clear your calendars for early January."

"I dunno," Jude said. "I might be booked."

Aunt Kitty elbowed him in the ribs. "You most certainly won't be."

"You're right," Jude said and his smile was wide and genuine as he raised a mug of cocoa. The family followed suit.

"Congratulations to the both of you," Jude said. "And welcome home, sis."

"I've got a present for the soon-to-be newlyweds," Levi said.

"Already?" Seth said in surprise.

"Yep. Since you're gonna stay local, how about we keep Bubbles and Pinky here?"

Nora's gulp was audible. "Oh, Levi. Thank you so much. I've been trying not to think about them going to Colorado."

"Thank you," Seth echoed.

"Weirdest wedding gift ever," Jude said.

Seth could not hold back any longer and he pulled Nora into his arms. He kissed her, wondering how his body could contain so much bliss. The horses shifted, setting their bells jingling, a sound that rose into the star-splashed night.

Yes, he thought. There really was nothing better than a Death Valley Christmas.

* * * * *

If you enjoyed this book, look for the other books in the Desert Justice series:

Framed in Death Valley
Missing in the Desert
Death Valley Double Cross
Death Valley Hideout

Dear Reader,

Woo-hoo! Seth has finally gotten his happy ending and Jude's family is gradually being restored. I just love that, don't you? Set at Christmastime in the spectacular desert, this story strums all my happy notes. When I traveled to Death Valley on a research expedition, it was so much fun to learn about donkeys and donkey rescue. Did you know that donkeys in Death Valley are a non-native species? They can eat an average of 6,000 pounds of forage per burro per year! There are several agencies working to relocate these animaløs to mitigate environmental damage and care for their health. Closer to home, I found another rescue agency that provided some advice on the ins and outs of donkeys. Thank you to Zeb's Wish Equine Sanctuary in Oregon and God bless the work you do to rehabilitate special-needs equines. As always, I deeply appreciate you, my dear readers. Thank you for coming along on this fifth Death Valley adventure! If you'd like to sign up for my newsletter at danamentink.com, I'll keep you posted about the series and share some photos from my latest Death Valley excursion.

God bless!
Dana